Dubious Justice

M. A. COMLEY

New York Times bestselling author M A Comley

Published by M A Comley

Copyright © 2015 M A Comley

Digital Edition, License Notes

OTHER BOOKS BY

M A COMLEY

Blind Justice (Novella)

Cruel Justice (Book #1)

Mortal Justice (Novella)

Impeding Justice (Book #2)

Final Justice (Book #3)

Foul Justice (Book #4)

Guaranteed Justice (Book #5)

Ultimate Justice (Book #6)

Virtual Justice (Book #7)

Hostile Justice (Book #8)

Tortured Justice (Book #9)

Rough Justice (Book #10)

Dubious Justice (Book #11)

Calculated Justice (Book #12)

Twisted Justice (Book #13)

Justice at Christmas (Short Story)

Prime Justice (Book #14)

Heroic Justice (Book #15)

Shameful Justice (Book #16)

Unfair Justice (a 10,000 word short story)

Irrational Justice (a 10,000 word short story)

Seeking Justice (a 15,000 word novella)

Clever Deception (co-written by Linda S Prather)

Tragic Deception (co-written by Linda S Prather)

Sinful Deception (co-written by Linda S Prather)

Forever Watching You (DI Miranda Carr thriller)

Wrong Place (DI Sally Parker thriller #1)

No Hiding Place (DI Sally Parker thriller #2)

Cold Case (DI Sally Parker #3)

Deadly Encounter (DI Sally Parker thriller series #4)

Web of Deceit (DI Sally Parker Novella with Tara Lyons)

The Missing Children (DI Kayli Bright #1)

Killer On The Run (DI Kayli Bright #2)

Hidden Agenda (DI Kayli Bright #3)

Murderous Betrayal (Kayli Bright #4 coming June 2018)

The Caller (co-written with Tara Lyons)

Evil In Disguise – a novel based on True events

Deadly Act (Hero series novella)

Torn Apart (Hero series #1)

End Result (Hero series #2)

In Plain Sight (Hero Series #3)

Double Jeopardy (Hero Series #4)

Sole Intention (Intention series #1)

Grave Intention (Intention series #2)

Devious Intention (Intention #3)

Merry Widow (A Lorne Simpkins short story)

It's A Dog's Life (A Lorne Simpkins short story)

A Time To Heal (A Sweet Romance)

A Time For Change (A Sweet Romance)

High Spirits

The Temptation series (Romantic Suspense/New Adult Novellas)

Past Temptation

Lost Temptation

KEEP IN TOUCH WITH THE AUTHOR:

Twitter

https://twitter.com/Melcom1

Blog

http://melcomley.blogspot.com

Facebook

http://smarturl.it/sps7jh

Newsletter

http://smarturl.it/8jtcvv

BookBub

www.bookbub.com/authors/m-a-comley

This book is dedicated to my rock, Jean, whose love and devotion is my guiding light.

Special thanks to my wonderful editor Stefanie. Thanks also to my good friend Noelle Holten for her expert input, and of course, to Joseph, my superb proof reader.

Finally I'd like to thank Karri Klawiter for the superb artwork as always, you're a very talented lady.

PROLOGUE

Curiosity played a major part in his next movement. As he opened the door, it creaked its objection. Peering into the darkness, he ran his hand along the damp surface of the walls in search of a light switch. There wasn't one. Paul Lee turned, looking for his toolbox, and searched inside for a flashlight. He located it, but to his annoyance, it faltered on and off a few times before the batteries finally died. "Damn thing. I wonder what's in here."

He returned to investigate the opening. The door creaked again. A shudder rippled the length of his curved spine. Venturing farther into the small entrance, where his eyes were slow to adjust, he let his hands guide his way along the moist walls. Before long, he came to an abrupt halt. Once his eyes adjusted to the dark, he wondered if they were playing tricks on him. *A skeleton?*

A noise from behind disturbed him. *Shit! It's the owners of the house. If they find me in here...*

The woman called out, then he could hear her feet clomping down the wooden stairs. "I've brought you a cuppa..." Her voice trailed off. His heart skipped several beats when he heard her running back up the stairs.

Shit! She must have seen the door open. I've got to get out of here. In his haste to retrace his steps, he slipped on the wet floor. He grunted from the impact of his torso hitting the protruding rock-faced wall. Because he was distracted, the blow from behind came as a shock. Paul crumpled to the floor and covered his head with his hands, protecting himself from further blows. "Please, don't hit me again."

"Get out!" The man's harsh tone reverberated round Paul's confused and wounded head.

Paul struggled to his feet. Glancing at the entrance, he saw only the huge brute of a man blocking his path. *Stay cool. Don't anger him any more than he already is.* Paul eased out of the confined space, his hand still holding the back of his head. He could feel the stickiness of the blood oozing through his fingers.

The man's steely, angry gaze locked on to his. "What the fuck do you think you're doing in there?"

"I'm sorry. I was tracing a cable back through the wall. I thought it went into this cupboard. I was wrong. Please, I didn't see anything in there."

The man's stare intensified. His jaw moved as he ground his teeth. "Are you sure? I think you're lying to me."

"No, I swear. I saw nothing. It's too dark to see anything in there anyway."

The man stepped forward. The dreadful smell of the man's stale breath filled Paul's nostrils and warmed his cheeks when the brute said, "I don't like liars. Nothing good comes from telling lies. I've been surrounded by liars all my life, and not one of them has got away with it. Now... *tell me* what you saw." His lip twitched, curling up at one side to reveal the left half of his mouth and the rotten teeth hanging on by a thread.

"Nothing, I swear. Please, let me go. I won't tell anyone."

"Uh-oh, mistake number one. You said you saw nothing, yet you're not going to tell anyone. Tell them what? Answer me, *prick*. What did you see in there?"

His tone turned more menacing, along with the glare. Paul could feel his bowels loosening, and his body began to tremble. "Nothing. I need to go now. The job's finished anyway. My boss will be expecting me. He hates it when I return the van back to the yard late." Paul tried his hardest to come up with a plausible excuse to exit the situation, and the house. Truthfully, his boss didn't care how long his employees took to do a job, and they often took the vehicles home with them. That's how he was able to do his little jobs on the side, like this one. *Why the fuck was I so nosey? Why?*

The man's eyes narrowed. "You're a bull-shitting piece of dirt. Tell me the truth, or I'll shove you back in there and let you rot just like the other one."

Tears sprang to his eyes. He swallowed the lump of bile that had mysteriously formed in his throat. A picture of his happy family swept into his mind. "Please, sir. Let me go. I have a young family, a wife and children. They'll be expecting me home soon for my daughter's birthday party." *I hope he doesn't figure out I'm lying.*

"Yeah, I've heard all about them. You've been boring my wife senseless for days talking about how much you idolise them. You should have thought about your damn family before you started snooping in places that don't concern you. Now, fucking answer the question... what... did... you... see?"

Paul heaved a large sigh, as a sign of defeat. "A skeleton. Please, let me go. I swear again, I won't tell anyone about what's in there—I promise. Just let me go. My family needs me. My head hurts. I'm losing blood. I need to get to the hospital. Your secret will be safe with me. Just let me go, please?"

"Stop your whining. You're getting on my tits. Get your things together and get out of my fucking house."

Quickly, Paul gathered all his tools together under the man's watchful gaze, not caring if he left behind any of his prized equipment. All he wanted to do was get out of there, alive.

"There, I'm done. I'll call back in a couple of days for my money. There's no need to go to any bother paying me now." Paul's head was throbbing violently after bending down to collect his tools, but he kept his smile fixed firmly in place all the same. He extended his hand to the man, who slapped it away.

"Just get out of my house and don't come back. You hear me?"

Paul didn't need telling twice. He turned and marched towards the wooden stairs, wondering if the man's wife would be at the top to greet him. He didn't get very far before he felt the first whack on the back of his head. The excruciating pain rippled through his body and weakened his legs, knocking him off balance. He swung around, hoping his toolbox would connect with his assailant's face, and he cursed when he found he didn't have the strength to put any significant power behind his swing. He slumped against the wall and stumbled back down the two steps he'd taken. "Please. No more."

In spite of his begging, the blows continued, intensifying in strength and frequency until neither his head nor his body could take any more. Even curling into a foetal position couldn't offer the protection from the man's strikes. It didn't take him long to work out the man wouldn't stop until he'd taken his last breath. The menacing glimpse he'd caught in the man's eye made him aware of that fact.

The final image that filled his mind was the day he'd stood in church, marrying his childhood sweetheart. *I love you, Jess, and our kids. Go on to find another man who will take care of you the way I have. Never forget me, my love. Never forget how much I love you all...*

CHAPTER ONE

Lorne and Charlie each wrapped an arm around the other's waist and sniffled. Apart from the box of toys they'd placed in the cupboard under the stairs, the newly dug grave was to be all that would remind them of their dearly departed pet dog, Henry. "He was loved every day of his life, Charlie. Never ill-treated, that's all a dog ever wants in his life, to be treated with kindness, love, and respect. He'll always be remembered, and once this tree grows, I'll get Tony to build a seat around it and we'll both be able to come and sit out here with him to contemplate the world and all its failings."

"How long will that be, Mum?"

Lorne pulled her close and kissed her daughter's forehead. "The man at the garden centre said that sambucas grow rapidly after a couple of years. I need to prune it in half for the first year or two to ensure the bark thickens before it really takes off. I'll get a plaque made with Henry's picture on it. We can attach it to the bark of the tree once it grows. How's that?"

"That would be great. I really miss him. How long does it take to get over losing an animal like this, Mum?"

"Everyone's grieving time will vary, sweetheart. Henry was different. You grew up with him. He wasn't just an ordinary pet to us, was he?"

"I thought if I said the same thing, you'd ridicule me."

"I'd never ridicule you for thinking like that. Come on. Let's go and see how Sheba is getting on." They walked into the kennels and approached the German shepherd's kennel. Sheba perked up immediately the second she laid eyes on them.

Charlie crouched, and the dog hurried to where she'd slipped her fingers through the cage. Sheba rubbed her head against Charlie's hand. "Have you thought any more about inviting her to share our home with us? It's not too soon, is it?"

"I don't see why not. Look at her—she's crying out for a new home. She's so attached to you now, and providing it's all right with Tony, I say we should integrate her into her new surroundings from today. Of course, we need to be mindful that she'll never replace Henry—no dog will ever do that—but having her trampling through the house will sure help ease the grief suffocating all of us at the moment."

Charlie rose to her feet and threw her arms around Lorne. Burying her head in Lorne's shoulder, she whispered, "Thanks, Mum. That's the best news I've had in days."

Lorne patted her daughter on the behind then brushed the tears from both their cheeks. "Right, I better get off to work now, love. Are you going to be all right? Tony will be sticking around here this morning. He and Joe have arranged to meet a prospective new client this afternoon."

"Go, I'll be fine. Do I have permission to introduce Sheba into the house while you're at work? I promise not to neglect my chores around the kennels."

They made their way back through the kennel and out to Lorne's car. "I trust you. Of course you can. I think she'll need a bit of house-training, too. The sooner she learns that, the better. I'm sure she'll cotton on soon enough. She's a clever girl."

"Thanks, Mum. Love you." Charlie waved her off.

As Lorne drove into London to the police station, where she was a detective sergeant in the Metropolitan police force, her heart felt less constricted than it had in days since her beloved pet's death.

"Morning, all. How is everyone?" She called out as soon as she pushed through the swing doors of the incident room.

"Do you have to be so bright and breezy?" Katy queried with a frown. "Morning, by the way." The detective inspector was sitting in a chair next to her boyfriend, Alan Jackson, nicknamed AJ by the rest of the team. They both had their heads close to the computer screen on his desk. By the serious expression on Katy's face, Lorne had an inkling that her day was about to start off with a bang.

She pulled a nearby chair close to Katy then sat down heavily. "Okay, dare I ask what I'm supposed to be looking at?"

"Our next case. Which reminds me, we need to get over there ASAP. I was waiting for you to arrive. Don't get comfortable. I'll fill you in on the way."

"What are we waiting for?" Lorne stood up quickly, almost tipping over her chair.

Katy rushed into the office to fetch her jacket and handbag, and swept past Lorne on her return. "AJ, keep searching that CCTV footage until we get back."

AJ nodded. "Will do."

"Come on, Lorne. What's keeping you?" Katy shouted over her shoulder as she trotted out of the room.

Lorne shook her head behind her partner's back and raced to keep up with Katy as she made her way through the station like a mini-tornado. Once they were settled in the car and Katy had input the directions into the sat nav, she set the car in motion then told Lorne all about the scene they were on their way to.

"We got a call about a suspicious van parked up in a supermarket car park."

"Okay. What's suspicious about it?" Lorne queried.

"Apart from the engine running and a dead body, presumably the driver, being found inside the van, you mean?"

"Damn. Why was the engine running?"

"You'll see when we get there," Katy replied with a shrug.

Lorne spent the rest of the trip sporting an intensively creased brow while Katy kept glancing her way, wearing an amused grin.

The car park had been cordoned off with crime scene tape. An excessive amount of forensic and police cars were in attendance, too.

"This seems a little overkill. Why all the interest?"

"Not sure it warrants this amount of interest, by what I've heard. I'll send them on their way once we've looked over the scene ourselves."

They got out of the vehicle and walked towards the van. They flashed their IDs at the uniformed officer guarding the area, and he lifted the tape for them to duck under. As they approached the van, Patti, the pathologist, saw them arrive and smiled.

"Strange one this, girls."

"In what way, Patti?" Lorne asked.

"Generally, if someone tries to commit suicide in this way, they don't tend to do it in such a public area."

"Suicide? Is that how you're reading this, Patti?" Katy asked.

"Considering I've only been on the scene for the last half hour, yes, that's my take on the victim's death at this moment in time. Of course, that can change at the flick of a switch."

Lorne got closer to the vehicle to assess the scene for herself. She withdrew her plastic gloves from her pocket and snapped them on. "A hosepipe leading to the exhaust. Is that really the cause of death?"

"Like I've stated already, it appears to be the cause of death for now."

"I sense some doubt in your tone, Patti. Come on, give us the full picture. Where are your thoughts heading with this one?" Katy prompted the pathologist.

"The man was found in the rear of his vehicle. Usually, when someone decides to take their own life in this manner, they remain seated at the front of the vehicle, close to the end of the pipe, for greater impact to aid their demise."

"I see. I know you've recently arrived, but have you had a chance to get a close look at the victim yet, Patti? Is that what lies behind your doubtfulness?"

"Astute as ever, Lorne. I quickly surveyed the corpse and found a severe wound to the back of his head, actually quite a few wounds to his head. However, I think this particular one would have caused a major trauma."

"Mind if we take a look?" Lorne strained her neck to see the corpse for herself from the passenger door.

Katy pulled her back. "We need to be suited and booted before we get near the victim, Lorne. You know that."

"Yeah, I know, boss. I was just trying to take a sneaky peek."

"You can do that after we get togged up." Katy turned her back, and Lorne took the opportunity to pull a face at her partner.

She looked over at Patti, who'd spotted the insubordinate display and was suppressing a chuckle. Lorne's cheeks warmed, and she shrugged at her good friend.

Once they were dressed in white paper suits and blue shoe covers, Lorne and Katy squeezed into the back of the van to assess the body, under Patti's close supervision.

She lifted the corpse's head and pointed out the wound she had referred to earlier. "Here, you see?"

"Okay. Could it have happened on something already in the van, on one of his tools, perhaps?" Lorne asked.

"I can't really see anything lying around that would make a dent this size in his skull. Be my guest to look for yourselves," Patti replied, her hand sweeping the area, inviting the search.

Lorne examined the immediate floor area of the van, only to be disappointed by the result. "Hmm… I see what you mean. I take it you're suspecting some kind of foul play has gone on then, Patti?"

"At the present time, *I'm* not saying anything—*you* are. I'm not one for jumping to conclusions. You know that. Let's see what we find once we get the corpse back to the examination room."

Katy nodded. "I know where my line of thinking is heading on this one."

"What's that?" Lorne had a fair idea what Katy was going to say next.

"I think we're looking at a murder crime scene and not a suicide. Don't hold me to that, though."

"Interesting. So you reckon all of this has been staged. For what reason, I wonder?" Lorne nodded thoughtfully.

"That, dear ladies, is for you to find out," Patti stated unnecessarily.

CHAPTER TWO

Armed with the victim's ID, Lorne and Katy drove back to the station. Silence filled the car during their return journey. That was unusual for them.

When they arrived, Katy called for the team's attention, and Lorne took up her position by the board, ready to write down any clues they'd uncovered at the scene. Lorne wrote a name on the clean board: Paul Lee.

"Okay, gents and lady, here's what we have so far," Katy addressed the team. "Paul Lee was found dead in Morrison's car park this morning, with the engine to his work vehicle still running. A hosepipe attached to the exhaust had been pushed through a small gap in the window on the driver's side of the van."

"So it's a successful suicide?" AJ asked. The frown he wore showed it was more a dubious question than a statement.

"At first glance, the pathologist thought that we'd been called out to a mere suicide, but after studying the victim more closely, she's inclined to believe that we're looking at a murder. That is yet to be confirmed by Patti. It's the route we'll be taking from here, though," Katy said.

Lorne wrote the words *murder enquiry* at the very top of the board, and using a marker pen, underlined it with three heavy lines.

"So, this is what the plan of action is going to be today. First, I need an in-depth background check on the victim. Karen, I'll leave that in your capable hands, okay?"

Karen Titchard smiled in agreement and jotted the victim's name down in her notebook. "Yes, boss."

"Stephen, can you get me Paul Lee's employer's details? The firm is County Electrics. Lorne and I will visit the firm as soon as this meeting is over."

"Consider it done." Stephen swivelled in his chair and started up his computer.

"AJ, I'd like you to obtain and search all the relevant CCTV footage in that area. See if we can pinpoint a time Mr. Lee parked his vehicle and, more importantly, if anyone or another car was seen in the vicinity around that time. My betting is that you'll come up trumps on that one."

"I'm on it now," AJ said, tapping at the computer and studying his screen.

"All righty, that just leaves you, Graham. I'd like you to search the database for any similar crimes which may have occurred in, what? The past couple of years, I guess? Plus, can you also see if anything dodgy comes up in our records relating to County Electrics? It's a long shot. However, I'd rather discount them early on than waste our time on it later."

Graham gave a brief nod. "Yep, I'll hopefully get back to you with the info soon, boss."

"So, that leaves you and me, Lorne. I'll need to do my usual daily chore of trawling through the post first thing, but then I think you and I should visit the electrical firm once Stephen has completed his fact-finding mission. You could always tie up the loose ends on that burglary case we just finished. That would be a big help to me."

"Whatever you want me to do is fine. Leave it with me." Lorne disguised how upset she was not to be directly involved in the case from the outset. She didn't think Katy was intentionally keeping her out of the initial loop, but the fact that her partner had set her a task not related to the new case struck her in the chest with a ten-inch blade. As Katy turned on her heel and headed for her office, Lorne called after her, "Not trying to tell you your job or anything, but don't you think the man's relatives should be informed? His wife, for instance?"

"Damn, you're right. Okay, leave the other case. Can you sort out the details? We should pay his wife a visit—if he has one—first, before we go and see his boss."

"Yep, that's what I'd do."

Katy shook her head, then she turned and headed for her office again, leaving Lorne wondering if everything was well with her partner and dear friend. As Katy disappeared from view, Lorne made a quick detour to her desk via AJ's. "Everything all right with Katy, AJ?"

"As far as I know. She rang her parents last night and has been a little quiet ever since. I tried to find out what was wrong, but she clammed up, said it was personal."

Lorne cringed. If Katy ever said that to her, she knew how hurt she would have been to think Katy didn't trust her enough to confide in her. *Maybe something is wrong with her parents or even Katy herself.* Lorne knew how AJ must have felt, being her boyfriend. She patted him on the shoulder and winked. "Leave it with me. I'll get it out of her. Don't take it personally, okay?"

"I won't. I'll try not to anyway. Thanks, Lorne."

For the next half an hour, the office was filled with people either tapping their computer keys or contacting people on the phone. By the time Katy reappeared, Lorne had collated what information the team's combined efforts had produced. She presented Katy with the facts.

"Excellent work, team, very efficient. Let's hope the rest of the case goes as well. Lorne, can you quickly note down the details on the board, and then we'll shoot off. First stop will be to inform the wife."

"Okay. This will just take me a second to complete, and then I'll be ready for the off."

Katy headed back towards her office but stopped at the vending machine to buy a coffee. Lorne issued her a cheeky smile. Katy tutted and placed another coin in the machine. Lorne jotted down the rest of the information relating to the case then followed Katy into the office, closing the door behind her.

"Is everything all right? You seem a little distracted, and AJ mentioned you rang your parents last night."

"Take a seat. AJ's got a big mouth. Sorry, have I been snappy this morning? I hadn't noticed."

"Not particularly. Like I said, a little distracted. Should I be concerned? Want to share what's troubling you?"

"Something and nothing really. I rang Mum last night to see how they both are, and she was a little distant. Not sure if they've fallen out with me because I haven't visited them in a while or what."

"You're probably being overly sensitive about things and misread the signals. I'm sure your mum is all right really. It was probably your guilty conscience pricking you, that's all."

Katy took a sip of coffee. "It was more than that. I wish I could get time off to go and see them. You know how hectic it's been around here lately."

"I know. I'm sure they realise how difficult it is for you to take time off to visit them, too. Do you have any holidays left?"

"Left? I haven't used any of my entitlement for this year yet. I can't seem to plan anything."

"You've got to use them up, Katy. Use them or lose them, as the saying goes."

"I know. Time goes so bloody quickly around here. I didn't even use my quota for last year."

"You're kidding! Don't start treating the job as a crutch, Katy. You need your time off. Recharging the batteries is a no-brainer in our line of work."

"Hark at you! Of course, you've always taken your entitled holidays, haven't you?"

Lorne could feel the colour rise in her cheeks. "Umm... okay, you've got me by the short and curlies on that one. Hey, do as I say and not as I've done in the past. There's no way I'd go without my holidays nowadays."

"Why? Because you're older and wiser? Is that what you're telling me?"

"No. It's because I have a life now. Tony wouldn't let me neglect him anyway. Hey, you're in the same boat with AJ. You'd be foolish to neglect him, hon. He's head over heels in love with you. He's also concerned about you, so don't go taking it out on him."

Katy stared down at the desk and fidgeted in her seat for a second or two before she finally glanced up at Lorne with misty eyes. Lorne was immediately alarmed by her partner's demeanour. She reached across the table in search of Katy's hand.

"What's wrong, Katy? This isn't like you. What aren't you telling me, hon?"

Katy inhaled the deepest of breaths and exhaled slowly. "Maybe another time. We should get out on the road." Katy left her chair and walked past Lorne.

Lorne gently touched her friend's forearm. "I'm always available if you need a shoulder to cry on. You know that, right?"

"I know. I appreciate the offer. I need to come to term with the news myself first before I start spreading it around."

"Whoa! You can't leave me dangling like *that*?"

Katy shrugged. "I can, and I am. Come on. We have work to do. Give me time, Lorne. I'll tell you when I'm good and ready. Don't push me, okay?"

Lorne's mouth twisted, and she held her hands up in front of her. "Hey, pushy is one thing I ain't."

Katy laughed. "Crap, have you heard yourself?"

Incensed, Lorne grabbed her handbag off the back of the chair and ran after Katy. She caught up with her partner at the top of the stairs. "Are you saying I am? Pushy, I mean?"

Katy covered her chest with her hand. "No. I wouldn't dream of it."

Lorne's mouth gaped open, and she froze on the stairs mid-flight.

"It was a joke, Lorne. Stop being so sensitive. Time's getting on."

Lorne rushed to catch up with Katy again, and once she'd entered the address into the car's sat nav, she revisited the conversation in her mind during the course of the journey. *How dare she think that? I'm not pushy! Not in the slightest. Am I?*

"Here we are. I'll lead. You back me up if I give you the nod, all right?"

"As usual. Right, there's no need to treat me like a junior, Katy."

"Oh, have I hit a nerve? Is that what's with the snappy retort?"

"No. Not at all." Lorne raised her chin to dismiss any further challenges.

"Have you got the woman's name?" Katy leaned over the steering wheel and surveyed the semi-detached house in front of them.

"Yeah, Mrs. Lee."

"Ha, bloody, ha."

Lorne stifled a grin and got out of the car. "Yeah, Jessica. Looks a nice area."

"It does. I hope she's at home and not at work." Katy rang the doorbell.

A woman in her early thirties opened the door, balancing a toddler on her hip. She had the tell-tale signs that she'd been disturbed while cooking smeared across each cheek. "Hello? Can I help you?"

"Mrs. Jessica Lee? I'm DI Katy Foster, and this is my partner, DS Lorne Warner. Do you mind if we come in for a chat?" Katy showed the confused woman her warrant card.

"What's this about? I've done nothing wrong. Oh no… it's not Paul, is it?"

"Please, it would be better if we came inside to discuss this in private."

The woman left the support of the door and staggered backwards into the open-plan living room. There was another child around the age of three or four playing with coloured blocks on the rug.

Mrs. Lee hugged the little girl she was holding and called her other child to her. "Cara, come to Mummy."

"I'm sorry, Mrs. Lee, maybe it would be better if the children went with my partner?" Wide-eyed, Katy glanced at Lorne, obviously needing backup.

The woman hugged her children tighter. "Anything you have to say can be said in front of them. What is it?"

Katy motioned for Mrs. Lee to sit on the sofa. The woman did as instructed; one child on her lap. The other child settled on the floor, grasping her mother's leg as if she knew what was about to happen. "Mummy, who is this?"

"Hush, Cara. Let's listen, darling."

Katy heaved a deep sigh. "I'm sorry to have to tell you that your husband is dead."

The woman stared, lost for words. As the realisation set in, she kissed both the children on the head, then tears began to trickle down her colourless cheeks. "No. He can't be. Not Paul. He was fine when he left here yesterday. He can't be d…"

"Mummy, why are you crying?" little Cara asked quietly.

"It's all right, sweetheart. Mummy's had some bad news."

Lorne got down on the floor and started to build a house with the blocks.

Cara kissed her mummy's cheek and crawled across the floor to join Lorne.

The girl, snatched a red brick, then a blue one, from Lorne's hand. "These are my toys. No one touches my toys. You upset my mummy!"

"I'm sorry, Cara. Why don't you show me what you can do with these bricks, eh? I'm eager to build a house of my own. Maybe I'll be able to pick up some valuable tips from you if I watch carefully enough."

"Well, you put this one here…"

Lorne had been successful in her mission to distract the girl. She heard Katy let out a relieved sigh and lower her voice as she continued to speak to Jessica Lee.

"Again, I'm very sorry for your loss. Can you tell me when you last saw Paul?"

"Yesterday, about eight o'clock in the morning."

"And he hasn't been home since?" Katy asked. She withdrew her notebook from her pocket and took down her own notes since Lorne was preoccupied with the woman's daughter.

"No. He rang me last night, told me not to wait up for him as he had the chance to earn some extra money."

"On the side?"

The woman looked horrified by Katy's suggestion. "No, definitely not. Paul's an honest man… was… where did it happen? Was it a road accident? I've told him to be careful driving after working such long hours." She pulled a tissue from the box on the small table next to her, blew her nose, then using her other hand, swept her little daughter's hair back off her forehead.

"He was found in his van in a car park in town."

Jessica's brow furrowed. "I don't understand. What car park?" Her eyes widened as it appeared something had dawned on her. "Was Paul alone?"

Katy nodded. "Yes. I understand what you're implying, but in this case, we're not looking along those lines. Not unless you're saying we should be."

Jessica shook her head vigorously. "No. Paul loved me. Loved our children. In fact, when he wasn't at work, he spent all his spare time with the family. He'd never ch…" She paused briefly then covered her daughter's ears. "Get involved with another woman."

"I'm sorry to have to ask." Katy smiled at the woman. "Okay, I'm sorry this is very awkward, but the initial signs are, until a full post-mortem has been carried out, that your husband's death resembled a suicide." Katy lowered her voice to say the final word.

Jessica gasped. "No. Never. Paul would never do that—not to me, to us. Never."

"Like I say, that was only the initial findings. We'll know more in the next day or two. If we can rule the first option out, then I have to ask if you know of anyone who might have a possible grudge against your husband."

Jessica thought for a moment or two before she replied, "No. He's never been in debt. He certainly doesn't gamble or anything like that." She ran a hand over her face. "My God, I can't believe I'll never see him again." Tears she'd struggled to hold back for the sake of her kids sprang from her eyes.

Lorne glanced up at Katy. Her heart went out to the woman having to deal with such traumatic news in front of her children. If Lorne had been in Katy's shoes, she would have insisted that she share the news about the woman's husband's death alone, out of earshot of the children. Over the years, she'd very rarely witnessed this kind of situation going smoothly. *Why would it?* Hearing about the passing of a loved one is one of the hardest things to deal with in this life. No one can tell how a person will react when hearing such devastating words. Lorne left Cara and approached Jessica. She extracted the child the woman was cradling from her grasp and took both the children out of the room. Not long after, once she'd settled the confused girls into chairs around the kitchen table, she heard Jessica sobbing and saying her husband's name over and over again.

The heartbreaking incident went on for more than ten minutes. In that time, Lorne tried her hardest to distract the children, asking them what they liked to do best with their parents and about places they'd visited. Lorne found it hard at first, not having dealt with children as young as Paul Lee's daughters were in years, but then Cara made it easy for her to slip back into conversing-with-kids mode as she was a little chatterbox.

"Daddy takes me to the pool on Saturdays. He's teaching me to swim," Cara said, a huge smile lighting up her face.

"That's lovely, sweetie. Are you a good swimmer?"

Cara's head bobbed eagerly. "Oh yes, with my arm bands on."

"It's been ages since I went to the pool. Do you enjoy swimming, Cara?"

"Sometimes! Maybe not so much in the cold weather. In the summer, it's much betterer."

"Do all of you go to the pool, or is this little one too young for that just yet?"

"We all go. Mummy sits and watches. She hates the water. It scares her."

"That's a shame." Lorne's heartstrings tugged mercilessly at the thought of the kids' enjoyment being disrupted, now that their father was no longer around—yet another blow for Jessica Lee to deal with, unless another member of the family volunteered to step into her husband's shoes, and keep the children's swimming lessons going.

Katy appeared at the door to the kitchen. Lorne looked up and noticed her partner's sad expression. Katy did not usually show such emotion on the job. "It's time to go, Lorne."

Lorne rose from her chair, and Cara reached over and grabbed her wrist. "Lady, please don't go. I don't want to be here with Mummy on my own."

Lorne sat down again with a thump and held the little girl's hand in her own. "I have to go, sweetheart. Mummy will be okay. If you children are good for her, then it will help ease her pain more quickly."

"Mummy is upset, which makes me upset. I want my daddy. Where's my daddy?" Cara's tears cascaded down her plump, flushed cheeks.

Lorne and Katy just stared at each other, neither of them knowing what to do next. Thankfully a brighter-looking Jessica swept into the room to care for her children.

Katy cleared her throat. "Will you be all right, Jessica?"

"We'll cope, Inspector. I've just called my mum. She'll be over in half an hour."

"That's good to hear. Look, here's my card. If you need my help at all, don't hesitate to get in touch with me."

Jessica took the business card from Katy and placed it on the kitchen table. "Thank you. Just promise me that you'll keep me informed with your investigation and that you'll find whoever did this."

"You have our guarantee on that, Jessica."

Lorne and Katy showed themselves out of the home and walked in silence back to the car. Once inside, they both let out the heaviest of sighs.

Lorne spoke first. "How awful. Why would anyone kill a family man in such a manner? Why?"

"It's beyond me. According to Jessica, her husband had never had a cross word with anyone in his life. Hey, let's hold off on speculating too much about the case until Patti gives us the PM report, eh!"

"Yep, agreed. Where to now?"

"On to Paul Lee's workplace, I guess. Maybe we'll hear about a different side of the victim from his workmates. Who knows?"

Lorne very much doubted her partner's statement would hold much truth once they'd visited the company where he worked, but she lived in hope that some clue might surface once they started questioning his colleagues. It sometimes worked out that way.

CHAPTER THREE

The instant Lorne and Katy entered the reception area of the electrical firm, an angry voice emanating from the intercom confronted them. "Send him into the office the second he arrives. Got that, Susan?"

The woman behind the counter smiled uncomfortably at them and left her seat. "Sorry about that. I think he got out of the wrong side of bed this morning. He's not usually so grumpy. What am I saying? Yes, he is, but usually, his grumpiness generally takes place in private. What can I do for you, ladies?"

Katy and Lorne flashed their warrant cards. Katy introduced them. "DI Katy Foster and DS Lorne Warner. I take it that was the owner of the company we heard then?"

"Yes. That was Derek's dulcet tone you heard. Again, I can only apologise for him. Police? In connection with what, may I ask?"

"If it's okay with you, we'd prefer talking to Derek about that. Derek what, by the way?"

"Of course. Derek Wilson—he owns this place. I'll just check if he has time to see you."

"Thank you. Tell him to *make* the time. It's very important." Katy winked at the receptionist, who scurried across the room and knocked on her boss's door. They heard the man bellow, and the receptionist glanced warily over her shoulder at them.

Katy called out, "Tell him it's urgent and that he'll want to speak to us. He *needs* to speak to us."

The woman opened the door and closed it quietly behind her. Within seconds, she reappeared, looking somewhat flustered. She approached the counter, raised a section of it, and motioned for them to follow her into the office. "He's usually a pussycat, honest."

"We'll bear that in mind," Katy said with a sigh.

The door opened into an office that looked more like a storeroom, where a small desk was shoved into the corner of a room no larger than eight foot square in total. The receptionist tried to introduce them, but the boss glared at her and shooed her out of the room.

"Ladies, I'd offer you a seat, except there's no room for any. You wanted to see me? About what?"

"Mr. Wilson, we have some bad news for you," Katy began before the man interrupted her.

"Ha, go on, make this day even worse than it is already, why don't you?" He slammed shut a file he was working on and sat back in his chair. "Surprise me?"

"Maybe you'd care to share what's bugging you first, Mr. Wilson? Perhaps we can help you with that issue."

"I doubt it. Although, I do suspect one of my vans has gone missing. It would certainly save me a call to the coppers, er... I mean police to report the theft."

"Interesting. This van wouldn't happen to be in the hands of one of your men, would it?"

"Yeah, the guy neglected to bring the van back after work last night and hasn't showed up for his shift this morning, either. That's why I'm pis... fed up." His lips strained into a forced smile.

"That employee wouldn't be Paul Lee, would it?"

The man propelled himself forward in his chair. "Yes. Why? What do you know? He ain't used my van in a bloody armed robbery or anything like that, has he?"

"No, he hasn't. Mr. Wilson, it's with regret I have to inform you that Mr. Lee and your missing van were found in the local Morrison's car park early this morning."

"What the f... sorry, I don't understand."

"Then let me try and explain to the best of our knowledge. We received a call first thing this morning to say that there was a van with its engine running sitting in a car park. When our guys turned up, they found Paul Lee's body in the back of the vehicle."

The colour drained from the man's face. "Body? Are you telling me Paul is bloody dead?"

"Yes. I'm sorry if the news has come as a shock. The pathologist is carrying out an examination into the cause of death now. We're going to need to ask you and your staff some questions, Mr. Wilson."

"Call me Derek. Jesus, I can't believe it. Paul is usually the life and soul around here. A right prankster, he is. You'll not find anyone with a bad word to say against him, not round here anyway. You said the engine was running. How come?"

"We're not a hundred percent sure yet, but it would appear that the scene was set up to possibly look like a suicide."

"No way! No bloody way would that lad have committed suicide! That theory is beyond belief—well, to me, it is. Jesus, his poor wife. Does she know?"

"Yes, we've just come from there. As expected, the news was difficult for her to hear. Are you certain about the suicide aspect? Some people disguise their feelings or money problems well at work, in our experience."

"Not that bloody well. He loved Jess and the kids. Spent all day talking about how proud he was of them. That's why he was so popular with the customers, I suppose. He always came across as a proud family man. People seemed to sense that he was trustworthy. He'd never end his own life. He had too much to live for. Only last week, he booked time off to take his young family away in May. Kept saying this would be their first holiday together. How many people would go and do that if they were intending to top themselves, tell me that?"

Katy and Lorne glanced at each other. The man was right. Paul's behaviour didn't tally with someone intent on ending their life.

"I agree. That does seem to be out of the ordinary," Katy said, then she asked, "Would it be all right if we questioned your other employees, just to see if there was anything going on that you weren't aware of?"

"Go for it. They'll tell you the same. I'm sure of that," Derek said emphatically.

"Is there somewhere we can interview the staff perhaps?" Katy surveyed the messy office.

"Not in here. I need to get on with work. End of the month is a nightmare time for paperwork duties. There's a small canteen across the yard you can use." He rose from his chair and walked towards the door. "Come, I'll show you."

They followed him back through the reception area and out across the yard. The man constantly shook his head in disbelief, running a hand through his thinning grey hair as he walked in front of them. "Gather around, gents," he shouted to a few of his men loading equipment into the back of two vans.

"Boss, we ain't got time. The customer will be expecting us."

"Ged, get the fuck in here *now*. I ain't messing, boy."

Lorne heard the young man curse under his breath, then the tools he'd been shifting clattered onto the floor of the van. His insubordination earned him a glare from Derek just before he opened the door into the tiny porta cabin.

"This'll do," Katy said.

Ged and his colleague joined them and threw themselves into a couple of chairs. Derek, obviously peeved by the men's attitudes, flung his arms in the air and marched out of the cabin. "I'll leave you to share the news with them," he shouted over his shoulder.

Ged crossed his bulging arms across his puffed-out, erratically pumping chest. "What's this about, and who are you?"

Katy flashed her warrant card at the two men, who were both in their mid-twenties. "I'm DI Katy Foster, and this is DS Lorne Warner of the Met. First of all, can I say it would be a help if you gave us some slack. Your attitude sucks."

"Police? Why? What's going on? Has Old Man Wilson been fiddling the books or buying dodgy electrical wiring?"

"If you stop asking dumb questions long enough, I'll tell you," Katy said, adding a tut at the end of her sentence.

"All right, keep your panties on, lady. We're listening."

Lorne stifled a chuckle when Katy tutted a second time for the man's benefit. Over the years, she had encountered her fair share of mouthy pests like him. She knew it was all bravado for his pal's sake. "Hey, mate. Do us all a favour and listen with your ears and not that big mouth of yours. No one is in trouble. We're on a fact-finding mission, all right?" Lorne said.

"Yeah, all right. And I said, we're listening. Come on then," Ged said, giving them both a tight smile.

Katy continued, "First, I need to give you some bad news. Your colleague Paul Lee is dead. There's no easier way of putting it, I'm afraid."

Ged's arms dropped down to his sides, and his head jerked forward. "He's *what*? He can't be. He was only in here yesterday, larking about. What's he died of?"

"Shut the fuck up, man, and listen, will ya?" His colleague punched Ged lightly on the top of his arm.

Ged held his arm, snarled at his mate, then muttered, "Sorry. Go on."

"Okay, at the moment, we're thinking along the lines of a suicide."

Ged sat upright in his chair and shook his head. "No frigging way. Not in a month of bloody Sundays would that guy take the easy way out."

"Suicide, the easy way out?" Katy questioned. "Is that what you think?"

"Figure of speech, lady. Either way, Paul wouldn't stoop to that."

Katy folded her arms and leaned against the cabinet behind her. "Well, until the results of the post-mortem come back, that's all we have to go on. Derek seems to think Paul is a genuine family man. Is he—sorry *was* he? Some guys just give that impression to their workmates, when deep down, they're being ripped apart by guilt."

"Guilt? What did Paul have to feel guilty about? You're way off the mark with this, lady," Ged assured them adamantly.

"What the inspector is asking is whether Paul was having some kind of affair behind his wife's back," Lorne jumped in quickly.

"That's insane. No man could love his wife more. I'm telling you, he loved every hair on his wife's and children's heads. He'd never kill himself and leave them in the shit. Never."

"Okay." Katy smiled at Ged. "I get the point. Then the only other option that we will need to consider is that the crime scene was staged somehow, to look like a suicide. In that case, I need to ask you if someone might have had a grudge of any kind against Paul?"

The two men glanced at each other, looking confused. Then Ged said, "Nope. Not that I can think of. Paul was liked by everyone around here. Never fallen out with anyone, as far as I can remember."

"What about you? Anything ring a bell with you—sorry, I didn't get your name?" Katy asked the other man.

"Mo. It's Morris, but I hate that name. Nope, never seen Paul have even a slight disagreement with anyone around here."

"Thanks. What about on site somewhere? Pressures of the job, timescales to adhere to can lead to fractious times between the trades on a site, can't it?"

"Yeah, sometimes, but never with Paul. *Everyone* got on well with that guy!" Mo insisted.

Lorne shook her head. "Really? Nothing at all?"

"Nope," Ged said again. "You know that programme on BBC, the *Big Build*? The little electrician guy on there—what's his name? Billy, I think. Paul was very much like him, joked around a lot of the time, but excellent at his work."

"Even pranksters obtain enemies," Lorne added.

"Nope, there was never any malice in the pranks he pulled. Everyone—and I mean everyone—saw the funny side of his jokes. Man, I can't believe this. It's only just sinking in." Ged buried his head in his hands.

"Are there any other members of staff that we should be talking to?" Katy asked.

"Nope, you're speaking to the whole workforce," Ged replied, wiping his face with his calloused hands.

Katy pushed away from the cabinet and shook hands with both men. "Okay, then I think our work is done here, gents. You can get back to work now. Thanks for sparing the time to talk to us and giving us a wonderful character reference for Paul. That will go a long way in helping us with our enquiries."

"So, what happens now with the case?" Ged asked, his brow wrinkled.

"We'll carry on searching, asking his close friends and relatives. Maybe they can shed some light on something you guys aren't aware of. Again, thanks for your help."

The four of them left the cabin together. Katy and Lorne hopped back in the car and exited the car park.

"Where to now?" Lorne asked. "It has to be murder, doesn't it?"

"I'd rather not jump to that conclusion just yet, Lorne. Let's see what Patti comes back with first. Shall we drop by and see her? I think we should."

"Why not? To be honest, I think even if we start questioning Paul's friends, I can see us coming up with the same result."

"Me, too, sadly."

Katy put her foot down on the accelerator and headed for the hospital, where Patti's mortuary was situated in the lower level.

After dressing in the protective clothing, Lorne and Katy walked down the stark-white hallway towards the examination room, where they knew Patti would be, having just passed her office to find the door ajar and the inside empty.

Lorne knocked on the portal window. Patti looked up from the corpse she was cutting open and beckoned them into her theatre.

"Hello, ladies. You're just in time. Gather round if you will while I make the Y-section."

"Crap, Patti. We were hoping you would have finished this by now." Lorne adjusted the mask around her mouth to lessen the impact of the smell she knew was about to overwhelm her.

Lorne took up the position nearest to the pathologist while Katy kept her distance. "We're ready. Begin when you like," Lorne said.

"Thanks, that's kind of you. Right, I'll just do this and then show you what I found," Patti said, her scalpel poised at Paul Lee's clavicle.

Katy placed a hand over the corpse's chest. "Wouldn't it be better to tell us of your findings before you open him up?"

"Perhaps you're right. Okay." Patti tilted the body on its side to expose the wound on his head. "We've already established at the scene that I believe this is the COD. Well, I can now confirm that to be the case without the added need for a full post on the man. But you're aware of the law as much as I am that I need to fully back up the proof. This wound is far too deep to not have killed the victim immediately."

"Any idea how the injury occurred or what made such a large indent in the man's skull?" Lorne asked, taking a closer look at the wound as Patti pulled the hair and skin apart.

"Something sharp, I'm guessing."

"Sharp, as in a knife? Can someone stab someone in the head like that?" Katy asked, her eyes looking perplexed above the blue mask she was wearing.

"With enough force behind it, anything is possible, Katy," Patti said. "The thing is, my guys didn't find any likely items at the scene that could have been regarded as the weapon."

"Strange. Do you think the killer took it away with them as a trophy?" Lorne asked. She surveyed the wound even more closely, hoping to find an impression in the skull that Patti might have overlooked.

Patti lowered the body back onto the metal table and shrugged. "Who knows? Especially nowadays. Have you got any suspects in the case yet?"

"Give us a chance, Patti. What we have learned is that he was a well-thought-of chap. No affairs, discreet or otherwise, we should be delving into. No enemies from what we can tell, either. Very mysterious indeed," Katy said.

"Maybe he was in the wrong place at the wrong time then. But if that was the case, why stage the scene to look like a suicide?" Patti replied thoughtfully.

"Because the police don't tend to delve into suicide attempts, do they?" Lorne said.

"Good point, Lorne. Okay, let's get this over with. You'll notice a fair amount of bruising to his upper chest area as well as on his back. My thinking is that he might have been jumped on, beaten, perhaps a robbery that went wrong even."

Lorne tapped a finger against her nose. "Hmm... possibly. But surely if robbery was the motive, wouldn't the assailants have stolen the vehicle, instead of leaving it running? Just a thought."

"A good one at that," Patti was quick to agree. Then she sank the scalpel blade into the man's body.

"Did you go through his personal effects? Was his wallet still with him?" Katy asked, thinking along the same lines as Lorne.

"His wallet was in the back pocket of his jeans, along with his other ID. I guess we can discount robbery in that case, given the evidence left behind," Patti told them. She pulled the blade down the length of the man's breastbone to his belly button then withdrew the blade and dropped it into the waiting metal dish on the stand beside her.

"It's all very perplexing. No known enemies that either his wife or his work colleagues can tell us about. The vehicle left running instead of being stolen. The fact that someone went out of their way to stage this as a suicide. Why would anyone want to do that?" Lorne asked.

"Like I always say, when you ask questions about the motive to a crime, Sergeant, I can give you all the information, except that. It looks like you're going to have to dig deep to find the answers on this one." Patti picked up the scalpel again and started slicing off pieces of the victim's internal organs and depositing each piece carefully into sample pots so they were ready for more thorough tests. It was almost an hour before Patti finally let out a huge breath. "Well, that's it, ladies. Job complete."

"And? What's your professional opinion?" Katy asked.

"As it was in the beginning, Inspector, the blow to the head is the cause of death. He was dead minutes before any of the fumes from the exhaust could do any further damage. His lungs are clear in that respect."

"Okay, so now we have a murderer on the loose who kills innocent people by stabbing them in the head. Should be easy to find, eh?" Lorne said sarcastically.

"Maybe we're looking for someone who's just been released from a mental institute," Katy offered.

"Bit extreme, but I suppose anything is possible. Shit like that is always showing up in news bulletins nowadays. Are there any mental hospitals around the crime scene?" Lorne replied.

Katy shook her head. "Not a clue. Even if there aren't any in the area, it's still something we shouldn't discount. Any similar incident in the past has involved these people being set free—just shoved out the door with little or no money to their names—and never into the hands of an accompanying member of their family, from what I can remember."

"You're right. It's dreadful, these people who—let's be frank—are crying out for help, are neglected in such a way in today's caring society."

"Ladies, as much as I'd love to stand around listening to you debate what kind of killer you're after, I'm going to have to get changed and onto the next PM. So if you'll excuse me." Patty motioned for Katy and Lorne to leave the examination room.

"Oops, sorry. We ought to be getting back to the station anyway. Thanks, Patti," Katy said as they all left the room together. "We'll be in touch if we need anything else."

"Sure. Toodle pip, ladies, and good luck. You're going to need it."

CHAPTER FOUR

In spite of their best efforts, the team had not come up with anything significant in their absence, either. Katy left Lorne to run through what each member had uncovered, while she tackled the paperwork threatening to bury her alive in her office.

"Nothing on the CCTV footage, AJ, I take it?" Lorne asked, crossing the room to the sergeant's desk.

"I can show you what I managed to dig up. It's not much." AJ pounded the keys on his keyboard then pointed at the screen. "Here, look at the time in the top right. Three a.m."

"Is that significant, AJ?"

"When was the van found? Around five-ish? That means the engine was running for over two hours, and no one else noticed it in that time?"

"Let's be fair. It's not as if there are a lot of folks lingering in the streets at that time of morning, thankfully. Can you imagine the shit uniform would have to deal with if that was the case?"

"I suppose so," AJ admitted.

"Run the disc for me." Lorne leaned in, trying to make sense of the fuzzy image. "Not the best picture in the world, is it?"

"Nope, I doubt if I'll be able to clean it up, either. Wait—see what happens in a few seconds."

Lorne screwed up her eyes and got even closer. She could make out two figures at the base of the screen. "What are they up to? Do you think they're the killers?"

"Looks that way to me. That's nothing. Keep watching."

Lorne shuffled to the edge of the chair and watched the two figures—she was unable to work out if they were both men or not—carry what appeared to be a rolled-up rug and throw it into the back of the van. The two figures then disappeared from sight and emerged from the van a few seconds later, carrying the rug under their arms, looking smaller than it had before. "So they dumped the body and then removed the rug. Interesting. Can you tell if the engine is running at this point, AJ?"

"It isn't."

"Do we have footage of the van actually arriving? Can we make out who was driving from that?"

"Sorry, I should have said. The van arrived. One of these guys was driving it. The other one travelled in the dark vehicle off to the left."

"How strange! I wonder why they didn't shove the body in the back of the van before they arrived at the scene. Why take the risk of having trace evidence being left behind in the other vehicle? What's that all about?"

AJ shrugged. "It does seem odd. There's no point doing a thorough search of the vehicle or the crime scene then. Is that what we can gather from this?"

"I wouldn't say that. Some form of DNA might be found at the scene. We shouldn't give up hope on that front, AJ. Let's see what happens next… now they're rigging up the hose to the exhaust pipe. I'm getting the impression that we're dealing with professionals here, aren't you?"

AJ turned sharply to look at Lorne. "As in contract killers?"

"I don't think we can rule it out. If not contract killers, certainly people who have killed before. They're confident about their next movement. Not concerned in the least about leaving trace evidence in the car already. Pure arrogance, yes?"

"What's this?" Lorne hadn't heard Katy approach.

AJ explained what they were watching.

"Crap, it's not very clear. Can't you do any better with the image, AJ?" Katy asked, straining her eyes at the dodgy image.

"Nope, believe me, I've tried. The best thing we can do is send the disc off to the forensics lab, see if they can define the pictures better for us. Other than that, there's no hope of catching these bastards, using what we have here. No judge will accept crap images in a conviction."

"Okay, can you sort that out ASAP?" Katy asked, shaking her head in disappointment. "So they pulled up in two cars, took the body out of the boot of the car, and tossed it into the back of the van. It doesn't make sense."

Lorne nodded. "Yep, that's what we were just saying. Why? There must be a good reason, but what?"

"I know it's dark, but did the camera pick up any of the plate on the car?" Katy asked.

"Nothing. Not even a single digit."

"All right. You know what I'm going to say next, don't you, AJ?"

"I can hazard a guess. You want me to check all the footage in the immediate area and try and locate the van and car, yes?"

"Yep. The sooner we get the answers, the better, too. I agree with you both that these suspects seem like hardened criminals. What's more, I think Paul Lee wasn't as innocent as everyone makes him out to be," Katy suggested.

"Really? You think he's been doing dodgy business?"

"What else do we have to go on at this point, Lorne?"

"And where do we start?" asked Lorne. With very little clues to go on and stunning character references blocking their way, she didn't know where on earth they could turn to find anything of use to their investigation.

Lorne couldn't remember stumbling across a case as perplexing as this, not for a very long time anyway. Usually, something sparked the investigation off in the right direction—rumours of an argument, something, anything along those lines. But so far, they hadn't come across a single clue.

"What are you thinking, Lorne?" Katy asked as they walked back to Lorne's desk.

"I wasn't really. Just how flummoxed we are, I suppose. What do we do next? Wait for clues to drop into our laps? They're going to be from a very large height from what I can tell."

"I'm sure something will show up soon, Lorne. Until then, we need to just keep digging. Why don't you try and access Lee's bank account? If he's into drugs or dodgy dealings, it might show up there. Again, if not, then we're screwed."

"I'll get onto it now."

Katy called across the room to the other member of the team proficient at doing background research when the need arose. "Karen, look into Lee's employment history, see what that tells us. Will you please?"

"Searching for anything in particular, boss?"

"Not really, anything and everything that raises your suspicions, okay?"

"Rightio."

The afternoon drifted by slowly as the team worked away, searching for clues that turned out to be impossible to find. All facts led to Paul Lee having an exemplary record at his previous posts, all as an electrician. Lorne delved into his bank account, which again, didn't throw up any real surprises. He had regular salary payments going in and plenty of household standing orders going out, with one large payment of five grand to a local travel agent—the Lee family had recently booked a holiday to take place the coming May.

Lorne arrived home, feeling a little despondent, but her spirits soon lifted when she pulled into the drive and saw Charlie playing with their new family member, Sheba. The German shepherd was barking as it chased after the football Charlie was kicking the length of the paddock, where she exercised all the dogs during the day.

"Hey, it looks like someone is having fun," Lorne called over, interrupting their game.

Charlie beckoned for the dog to join her then came toward her mother. "Isn't she wonderful? She's going to be so good to train, Mum. I'm going to start her on the assault course soon. I think she'll be a class-A student, don't you?"

"What a great idea. Hey, if she proves good enough, you could consider entering a few of the local shows. Hey, you could even end up at Crufts. That would be terrific to have an agility champion in the house."

Charlie giggled. "Easy, tiger. Let's get her used to the equipment before we start planning our magnificent future. Don't forget, I have this place to run, too. Or are you insinuating I have a lot of spare time on my hands?"

Lorne's eyes flew open. "Never in a million years. I know how hard you work, darling. Are you coming in now?"

"It depends."

Her eyes narrowed. "On what?"

Charlie ruffled the fur on the panting dog's head. "On whether you're expecting me to get involved in preparing dinner with you or not."

"You cheeky mare. I'm sure Tony and I can conjure up something for dinner without your help. Has he been home long?"

"About an hour or so. He looked pretty excited about something, refused to tell me what it was until you got home. I'll stay out here with Sheba for the next twenty minutes if you like, to give you two a chance to discuss things. How's that?"

"You're a treasure." Lorne stretched over the fence and kissed her daughter's cheek. Then she walked across the drive and into the house, where she found Tony sitting at the kitchen table, surrounded by notes. "Hey, what's going on here?"

He lifted his handsome face, and a large smile welcomed her. Tony pulled out the chair beside him. "Come and join me."

Lorne approached the table, hooked her handbag on the back of the chair, and kissed him. "You look busy. Umm... don't you think we should get dinner out of the way first? I'm starving."

"It's all in hand. Dinner will be ready in half an hour. Just enough time for me to tell you about my latest case."

"Really? What culinary delight have you prepared, may I ask?"

"Fish fingers, chips, and peas."

"Wow, you really know how to spoil your adoring wife, don't you? Glad to see the romance is still alive and kicking in our relationship."

"I know. Don't get too used to being spoilt, though, will you? It took a fair amount of effort on my part to prepare that meal."

Lorne grinned. "I can just imagine the taxing skills it must have taken pulling open a bag of chips and wrestling with a box to set those breadcrumb-coated fish fingers free."

"I see your sarcastic gene is fully functional today, as always."

"Any chance of grabbing a coffee before we get stuck into this project?"

"Sit. I'll make it. It's certainly an interesting case, if Joe and I choose to take it on, that is."

"Why the hesitation? You can't afford to be fussy which cases to take on or not, can you?"

"I know that. It's just there might be an alternative reason to this case. Let me make your drink, and then I'll go over the story."

Lorne picked up one of the sheets of paper and read it. *Missing. Stag night.* Tony placed a welcome mug of coffee on the table and took the note from her hand.

"Nosey!"

"Yep, you knew that the day we met. Go on, tell me about the case. I take it a man has gone missing whilst out getting rat-arsed on his stag do, right?"

"That sums it up pretty well. Don't get me wrong. I'm excited about the case. We just hear so many of these kinds of things that end up just being the future grooms getting cold feet at the last minute, as though it's suddenly dawned on them that in a few days, they'll be giving up their freedom to marry one person."

"I'm hearing you on that, Tony. The thing is, you have to treat each case differently. You have to learn not to tar everyone with the same brush."

One of Tony's eyebrows rose. "I hate to remind you, love, but I'm in my forties now, not some wet-behind-the-ears teenager starting out on his first career."

"Sorry, gosh, really? Are you that old? Teasing! You know what I mean. I didn't intend it to come across as condescending."

Tony shuffled through the pages and picked out another note. "Anyway," he said, brushing aside her latest statement, "when I got back home, I did a quick search on the computer and came up with a surprising statistic. Over thirty men went missing in the UK alone last year during a so-called 'fun night out.'"

"Wow, that's interesting. Did it say how many of those men showed up again after a few days' absence?"

"More than two thirds. A couple of men were found dead, which came as another surprise to me."

"Accidental deaths? Like walking in front of a passing bus? Something along those lines?"

"Yes and no. One man ended up drowned in a canal," Tony replied, referring to his notes once again.

The alarm sounded on the oven, and Lorne stood up to look at the contents. "I guess you have a lot of background checks to make before you can start looking for the chap in question."

"Yeah, that's what I thought. How's dinner looking?"

Lorne grinned back at him. "Well done. Can you clear the table? I think if I leave it in here much longer, it'll be cremated fish and chips."

Lorne closed the oven door again and turned the temperature down to fifty degrees from the two hundred and fifty Tony had it on. It was far too high in the first place. Then she bellowed out the back door for Charlie to join them.

"Goodie, I could eat a horse, figuratively speaking, I mean. Not seriously," Charlie said when she and the panting Sheba entered the back door.

Lorne looked down at the charred offerings she was in the process of dishing up and chuckled inwardly. *I think you might want to reconsider that once this is put in front of you, Charlie.*

Tony seemed a little sheepish when Lorne placed the meals on the table. His eyes drifted from plate to plate. "I guess I messed up again. Big time, eh?"

Lorne and Charlie glanced at each other and burst out laughing. "Shall I get the takeaway menus?" Charlie asked, just barely succeeding to form the words in spite of sniggering uncontrollably.

"I'll get them." Dejected, Tony left the table and returned with their usual selection of menus. He had the world's significant culinary delights fanned out in his hands. "Any preference?"

Lorne pushed her plate away and took the menus. "Anything edible is preferable to this."

"I don't mind if you bar me from the kitchen in future," Tony said, the twinkle resurfacing in his eyes.

"Yeah, that's what I thought you'd say. Deliberate act, was it? Just so I don't ask you to cook in the future, which by the way, I didn't ask you to do tonight."

"Would I do such a thing?"

"Hmm… keep doing things like that, and I'll start to wish you'd gone missing on *your* stag night. Just saying."

CHAPTER FIVE

The Lee case progressed slowly for Lorne and the team. For the week, they busied themselves with a few smaller cases since the clues were somewhat limited. Despite their best efforts to dig deep into Paul Lee's background for any possible vendettas *et cetera* against the victim, nothing showed up at all. The CCTV footage had proven to be inconclusive, too. Yes, they had located Paul's van on the cameras in the vicinity of the crime scene, but the number plate on the other car, which they were desperate to find leads on, had been covered at all times. Lorne came to the conclusion that something altogether far more sinister was going on with this case. She just didn't know what—yet.

The phone on the desk rang, interrupting Lorne's train of thought. "DS Lorne Warner. How can I help?"

"It's the desk sergeant, ma'am. I have a chap at reception reporting that he's seen what looks like a dead person in a vehicle. Can you come down and see him?"

Lorne scraped her chair and tipped it over in her haste. "I'm on my way." She slammed the phone down and ran into Katy's office. "Sorry, I'm just going downstairs. A member of the public has spotted a dead person in a vehicle. I just wanted to give you the heads-up on it."

"Anything else?"

"Nothing yet. I'll go and see what he has to say."

Katy nodded. "Let me know if you think he's genuine and not a crank, and I'll get the relevant units to attend the scene. We need to be a bit cautious, though. They might think the person is dead, but the individual could be passed out or drunk."

"Yep, that was my first thought, too. Why didn't he ring 999 instead of turning up here to report the incident in person? I'll let you know."

Lorne sprinted through the incident room and down the stairs to the reception area. The desk sergeant pointed out the worried-looking man. "Interview Room One is free if you want to take him in there, ma'am."

"That's great. Can you arrange a cup of coffee to be sent in?"

Lorne opened the security door and introduced herself to the man. "Mr. Jordache, I'm DS Lorne Warner. Please come this way."

"Am I in trouble?" the man's voice quivered.

"No, it's just far more private through here. Unless you want to run through what you've found out here? The choice is yours entirely."

"No, I'll come. I can't be long though. I have a dentist appointment in thirty minutes. All I wanted to do was report what I'd seen. I don't want any trouble, miss."

"You're not in any sort of trouble, Mr. Jordache." Lorne showed the man along the narrow hallway and opened the door to the interview room. After they were both seated, Lorne took out her notebook and asked, "Now, can you tell me what you've seen and where?"

"Right. I always take my dog for a walk in the mornings down by the river, weather permitting of course. No good going down there when it's been pissing down. Oops... sorry, I meant to say teeming down. There's a small car park down there. I suppose for fishermen to park—never really thought about it before. Anyway, Rosie and I got out of the car and walked past this parked car. Well, it's one of those minivans, really. You know, the type solo tradesmen use, not the big vans—the little half ones."

Lorne smiled at the man, whose fearfulness of being questioned in a police station was making him chunter on nervously. "Take your time. So, it was a small half-van, as I call it. And the man was where? In the driver's seat?"

"That's the weird part. No. He was sitting in the passenger seat."

"If you don't mind me asking, Mr. Jordache, how do you know the man was dead and not just having a sneaky forty winks?"

"His eyes were wide open. Do you think it was the exhaust fumes that killed him?"

Lorne's attention piqued immediately. "Hold on a second. Are you saying the vehicle was running and there was a pipe leading from the exhaust into the front of the car?"

"Yes. That was the scene exactly. I knocked on the window. I couldn't see much smoke inside, but I think the guy was definitely dead."

Lorne shook her head in disbelief. "Why didn't you ring 999 right away?"

"Because I don't have a mobile, and the station was just down the road. Thought it better if I reported the incident myself."

"Okay, I need to get some teams down there immediately. Can you hang on for five minutes?"

The man looked at his watch. "Time's moving swiftly, Sergeant. I'm going to have to leave soon."

"Can you call back after your appointment? Oh wait, that won't work, I'll be at the scene by then probably."

"No, I have to go on several errands after the dentist."

"Well, we'll need to take a statement. All right if I send a uniformed police officer round to see you later on today? This evening, perhaps?" Lorne asked, eager to get on with organising the rest of the teams.

"That's all right with me. Would much rather give a statement at home than here." He gave Lorne a tight grin.

Lorne took down the man's address and showed him the way back into the reception area. "Good luck at the dentist, Mr. Jordache."

"Thanks."

Lorne bolted up the stairs two at a time. Breathless, she barged through the door to the incident room and waved her notebook above her head. "I think we have another one, guys. It looks like the same MO."

Katy rushed out of her office. "Did I hear right? Another suspicious death? Where?"

Lorne steadied her breathing before she spoke again. "In a car park down by the river. We need to get someone over there ASAP. Stephen and Graham, can you get down there now?"

Katy nodded. "Yes, go. Let's get SOCO down there, too."

"I'm on it." Lorne rushed to her desk and rang Patti's number. "Hi, Patti. Looks like we have another murder, similar MO to Paul Lee."

Patti exhaled loudly. "Why haven't I been notified of this?"

"I'm notifying you now. The witness has only just informed us. Katy and I will be at the scene soon. Are you going to attend?"

"Of course. Give me the location."

Lorne rattled off the address and was surprised when Patti hung up on her. "I guess we'll see you down there."

Katy's brow twisted. "Everything all right?"

"Yep. I think Patti might have got out of the wrong side of bed, that's all. I'll ring SOCO, and then that's it. Are you ready to shoot off?"

"Five minutes just to tidy up a few loose ends, and I'll be free."

When Lorne and Katy arrived at the scene, Stephen and Graham were busy cordoning off the area. "Was the engine still running when you arrived, boys?" Lorne called over the second she left the vehicle.

Stephen nodded. "I opened the door to check for a pulse, but it was obvious the guy was dead before we got here. I switched off the engine and closed the door again."

"Can you see any other wounds on the victim?" Katy asked, slipping her small hands into a pair of latex gloves.

"I only took a brief look, boss. Nothing too obvious from what I could tell," Stephen admitted.

Lorne put on her gloves, too, and approached the vehicle. She cupped her hand against the back window and peered through the glass. A tool bag and copper piping filled the rear of the van. "I'm thinking he's a plumber," Lorne suggested.

"That would fit. First an electrician and then a plumber. A pipe running from the exhaust. It has to be the same killer, surely?" Katy scanned the area around them.

"Both victims found in public car parks, too. Obviously, the killer—or should I say *killers*, as in the CCTV footage—don't mind taking risks, judging by the brazen attempt to get rid of the bodies."

Lorne began to circle the vehicle, her eyes cast down at the gravelled ground beneath her feet, searching for clues.

"Come on, Patti. Get a wriggle on," Katy grumbled impatiently.

It was another hour or so before the pathologist and the SOCO team graced the scene with their presence. By that time, Katy had sent Stephen and Graham back to the station to begin the preliminary enquiries into the man's ID. She hoped they could get a head start by using his number plate since protocol had prevented them from touching the body before Patti arrived.

"Don't start on me, ladies. Blame the London traffic. One accident after another we've encountered on the journey over here. Right, what do we have here?" Patti placed her black bag of equipment on the ground.

"Looks like a similar crime to Paul Lee's murder. Initial checks show that he's possibly a plumber. No formal ID—we were waiting for you to arrive to establish that. If you can make that your first priority, Patti, we'd appreciate it."

"Sure. Let me dive in there and see what I can find. John, take photos of the corpse before I have to move him, please."

One of the assistants, dressed head-to-toe in a white paper suit and armed with an expensive camera, stepped forward to take numerous shots of the victim.

"We need to know if he has any other injuries on him, Patti," Lorne stated.

"I know my job, Sergeant. Let John carry out his job first, and then I'll get in there and examine the victim for possible wounds as well as try and find some elusive ID for you folks."

"Sorry for stating the obvious," Lorne apologised, her mouth twisting into a grimace.

Ignoring Lorne, Patti opened the passenger door to the van. Talking into her Dictaphone, she commenced her assessment. Katy and Lorne took a few steps back, aware that if the pathologist found anything significant she would call them to relay the news.

"Bingo. Lorne, Katy, here a sec," Patti shouted.

"What do you have?" Lorne asked.

Patti turned the victim's head to the side to reveal a bloody opening in the rear of the man's skull.

"The same as Paul Lee's," Lorne said, moving in for a closer look at the wound.

"That gives us what we need to combine the two victims then," Katy said.

"It would appear that way," Patti admitted. "This man has defence wounds on his right hand, whereas Lee didn't. I suggest he had an inkling he was about to be attacked but could do little to prevent the incident. I'll know more after the PM. Let's get you a formal ID on the man, shall we?" Patti twisted behind the corpse to search the back pocket of his jeans and withdrew the man's wallet. After flipping open the leather flap, she pulled out his driving licence. "Victor Caprini."

Lorne jotted the name down in her notebook. "I don't suppose there's an address in there somewhere?"

"Yep. According to this, if he hasn't moved house and neglected to inform the right authorities, it's 55 Tollpuddle Road."

"Okay, we'll get over there now; see if we can find any relatives at home. He looks around twenty-eight to thirty, yes?" Katy suggested.

Patti nodded. "I'd put him around that age, yes. I'll finish up here and get the body moved. My day is pretty clear. There's no reason why I shouldn't be able to fit in the PM this afternoon."

"The sooner, the better, as always, Patti. You're a star." Lorne patted the pathologist on the back before the two detectives headed for their car.

Katy let out a huge sigh once they were seated and buckled up. "Damn waste of a young life, for what?" She started the car and exited the car park.

"I agree. I doubt this will be the last, either. Two bodies in a matter of days doesn't bode well. If the killers are getting off on killing these men, who's to say where their game will end? Do you think it's sexual?"

"Where did that come from, Lorne?"

She shrugged. "Not sure. We're presuming from the disc footage that the two assailants were male. What if one of them is a woman? Supposing they were enticing these men into their homes with the intention of killing them? I don't know—pure conjecture on my part, of course."

"Maybe you've just got a warped mind," Katy admonished with a chuckle.

"Seriously, though. Maybe I'm just assuming that after what we've encountered over the years." Lorne pointed into the air and continued, "Look at that case involving Jade's psychiatrist a few years back. He virtually brainwashed the killer to do his murdering for him, didn't he? That was sexually motivated."

"You're right, as always. How is Jade, by the way? Has she got over your father's death yet?"

"Sometimes she's back to her old self, and then other days, she sits around crying all day. My heart goes out to Luigi and the boys. Walking a tightrope like that day in and day out can't be easy."

"Does she work? Maybe if she had something to occupy her mind every day, she wouldn't be in such a dire situation."

"Not really. She does the odd day of volunteer work now and again, nothing major. Luigi insisted that she should stay at home and raise the children herself."

"Yikes, that's not something I would like to do. I'd rather take a leaf out of your book about how to rear kids if having children ever cropped up on my agenda."

"Hmm… well, I wouldn't like to suggest to anyone how they should raise their kids. Hey, no one is more surprised at the way Charlie turned out than me. Especially after all she's had to contend with during her young life."

"She's strong, has your fighting spirit running through her veins. She's a credit to you, Lorne. Not many twenty-year-olds can shout loud and proud that they run their own successful business."

"Successful? As in bringing money in? I don't think we can label the rescue centre as being a grand success just yet," Lorne pointed out.

Katy followed the directions the sat nav voice issued and crawled along the road until she spotted number fifty-five. Lorne could tell that the area was well cared for by the way each of the gardens looked maintained. They walked up the path of the semi-detached house, and Lorne knocked on the door. They had to wait a few moments before a blonde woman in her mid-twenties opened the door to them.

"Hello, can I help you? And no, I don't need windows or my ears bashed by Jehovah's Witnesses. Thanks all the same."

Katy and Lorne produced their IDs. "Sorry, we're not sure of your name, miss, but we'd like a chat with you about a Victor Caprini. Do you know him?" Katy asked.

"Police? Yes, he's my fiancé. Is he in some kind of trouble?"

Katy glanced over her shoulder at the road. "If you don't mind, it would be better to discuss this inside, in private."

Shaking her head in puzzlement, the woman stepped into the house, leaving the front door open for Lorne and Katy to follow her.

Once the three of them had travelled the length of the house and were in the kitchen, the woman sat at the round onyx table and motioned for them to join her.

"Okay, you've got my attention. What's this about? Should Victor be here with us? I could call him."

"No. This is very hard for me to say, Miss…?"

"Please, call me Tammy."

"Tammy. It's with regret that I have to tell you Victor's body was discovered this morning in his van."

"Body? I don't understand?" Her trembling hand swept over her face.

"He's dead. I'm sorry."

"What? How? Where did the accident occur? When?"

"The thing is, Tammy, Victor's death is suspicious. It wasn't an accident—at least we don't think it was," Katy informed the distressed young woman.

Lorne's gaze drifted to the large fridge behind the woman's chair. A number of crayon pictures adorned the door, stuck up with multi-coloured magnets. *Shit! Another bloke with a young family.*

Tammy gasped and covered her face with her hands. In between heavy sobs, she asked, "I don't... understand... are you saying... he was killed by someone?"

"Is there someone we can call to be with you?" Lorne butted in and asked.

Katy gave her an apologetic look for not thinking to ask the woman that herself.

"My mother. Can I ring my mother?"

"Of course, or I can do it for you," Lorne volunteered.

The woman reached for the mobile phone lying on the table and punched in a number, then she handed it over to Lorne.

"Hello, darling. I was just doing my housework, and then I was going to give you a ring."

"Sorry, um... this is DS Lorne Warner. We're with your daughter at her home, sharing some bad news. I wondered if it would be possible for you to come over to be with her."

"Oh my! Bad news you say? About what?"

"About Victor Caprini. Can I tell your daughter to expect you soon?"

"Yes, I'll leave immediately. Is Victor all right?"

"We'll inform you of that when you get here. Please, drive carefully."

"I'll be ten minutes at the most."

The woman hung up. Lorne pressed the button to end the call, then she smiled at Tammy. "Your mum will be here shortly."

"Thank you. I can't believe it. Why? Why would anyone kill Victor? He's the sweetest man going. Never hurt anyone as far as I can remember. We were planning our wedding..."

"Damn!" Katy said. "You have our sincere sympathies. I'm sorry, but we need to ask a few questions. Are you up to answering them or would you rather wait until your mother gets here? Maybe Lorne can make you a cup of strong tea?"

"Yes, that would be good. Help yourselves to a drink, too. Do you mind waiting till Mum gets here? I don't suppose I'll be able to think straight at the moment."

"That's understandable," Katy said as Lorne left the table to fill the kettle with water.

Ten minutes later, the front door opened, and Tammy's mum bustled into the room. Mother and daughter flew into each other's arms.

"What is it child? What's wrong?"

"Victor's dead, Mum. He's dead."

Lorne saw the mother's legs weaken, and the woman almost toppled against the table. Lorne sprang to her feet and guided her to a spare chair next to her daughter. "Take a seat. We'll try to explain what happened, although it's not too clear right now."

Mother and daughter clasped hands and listened, both struggling to hold back the tears.

Katy cleared her throat. "This is what we know as of this moment. Victor was found in a car park down by the river. The engine of his van was running, and there was a hosepipe running from the exhaust into the driver's car window."

"What? Why?" Tammy queried, clenching her mother's hand tighter until her knuckles turned white.

"We think the murderer has set up the scene to look like suicide. Did Victor have any suicidal tendencies?"

Tammy snorted. "No. That sort of thing would never enter his mind. I can't believe you would ask such a thing. Tell them, Mum… tell them how much he loved me and the girls and…" She pulled one of her hands from her mother's in order to rub her belly. "This one," she added.

Shit! She's pregnant. Poor woman!

Katy's gaze met Lorne's then returned to the two crying women. "I'm so sorry. How many months are you gone?"

"Four. That's why we're in the process of arranging the wedding. Victor wanted us married before this little one arrived. That's not going to happen…"

Tammy's mother hugged her as a sob broke free. "There, there, love. Don't think about that now. Is there any chance this wasn't a suicide, Inspector?"

Katy nodded. "A few days ago, we were called to a similar scene. A tradesman—actually, he was an electrician—was found in a car park with his van running. We also found evidence that he was likely murdered. We think the murderer staged both crimes as suicides to throw us off the scent."

"So, you think they're connected? Is that what you're telling me? That my future son-in-law was killed by a serial killer?"

"I wouldn't exactly go that far, Mrs—sorry, I didn't get your name."

"Eleanor Keen. Call me Eleanor, please."

Katy continued, "There are an awful lot more tests to be carried out by the forensic team yet, but we really can't discount the possibility of a serial killer."

"But why? What's the motive?" Eleanor asked.

Katy gave the woman a quizzical look.

"My ex was a copper, years ago, so I know all the terminology and a little about the procedure you'll be working under."

"I see. I'm not trying to pull the wool over your eyes, Eleanor. The truth is, it's still too early to pinpoint the whys and wherefores on either of the cases. All we know is that there are a few aspects to both cases making us presume they're linked in some way. As to the motive, we're desperately seeking one, which is where you come in. Can you think of any reason why someone would single out Victor—*any* reason at all? It doesn't matter if you think the possibility is trivial or not."

Both women looked at each other and shook their heads.

"You'd know more about that than me, Tammy. Can you think of anything that has occurred out of the ordinary in the last few weeks or months?" Eleanor questioned her daughter gently.

"Like what? Victor has been working extra hours to help buy things for the baby and to put towards the wedding."

Katy inhaled a breath then asked, "Is it possible that the stress became too much for Victor?"

"Why ask that, Inspector, when you've just admitted that you're not treating this as a suicide?" Eleanor bit back sharply.

"Sorry, I have to ask. We're not definite about your fiancé being murdered yet."

Lorne noticed Tammy's gaze drop to the table. She was wringing her hands as if she wanted to say something but was too scared to.

Lorne covered Tammy's hand and asked, "Tammy, is there something you're neglecting to tell us?"

Tammy's eyes sparkled with more tears when she turned her head to look at Lorne. "I'm not sure. He was trying to right his wrongs."

Lorne frowned. "What do you mean by that, Tammy? What wrongs?"

The young woman slipped her hands from underneath Lorne's and slumped back in the chair. "I can't… what if whoever has killed him comes after me? Can *you* guarantee my safety? Can anyone?"

"If you feel you need any kind of protection, then, yes, we can provide it for you." Lorne glanced at Katy, who nodded. "Please, you must tell us what you know. It could save us days of endless research."

Tammy half-smiled at her mother. "Sorry, Mum. Victor had gambling debts."

Eleanor gasped and covered her mouth with one of her hands.

Lorne asked, "Okay, and do we know what kind of gambling, Tammy?"

"Gambling, gambling, I don't know. He kept it hidden from me for months, only told me a week or two ago."

"Did he gamble on the horses, football? You know, online gambling, betting? Or did he go to a club or casino and get involved in card games, Tammy? He must have told you that?"

"He didn't, and I was too naïve to ask. I heard the word *gambling* and hit the roof. He pretty much stopped talking to me about it there and then. I warned him that I wouldn't marry him unless he'd cleared his debts first."

"Tammy… why didn't you tell me, love?" Eleanor looked disappointed and struggled to keep a smile on her face.

"How could I tell you that, Mum? It was an impossible situation, one that I needed to handle myself. You've been so kind to us, I didn't want to burden you with this issue, too."

"A daughter's problems are never a burden on a mother, Tammy. You should know that."

"So, when did you give Victor the ultimatum, Tammy?" Lorne asked.

"A few weeks back. I think it was guilt that made him confront the issue in the first place."

"Guilt?" Lorne queried.

"Yes, guilt. He's been a bit funny towards me since I announced that I was pregnant. I knew there was something major wrong. I just couldn't put my finger on what it could be. I'm not one of these down-trodden women. I speak my mind when things are troubling me. I'd had enough of taking crap from him and gave him the ultimatum one Friday night. He broke down in tears. I was torn between kicking him in the... balls and throwing my arms around him. For the sake of the baby, I went with the latter option."

Katy coughed slightly, intimating that she was about to interrupt Lorne's line of questioning. "He must have told you what type of debt was involved? Did he mention how he intended to pay it back at all? To whom he was in debt to?"

"No. I told him to deal with it himself. Was that the wrong thing to do? Am I to blame for this?" Tammy wailed and buried her head in her hands.

"That's nonsense. Isn't it, detectives?" Eleanor's eyes pleaded with Lorne and Katy to pour water on her daughter's unnecessary blame on herself for her partner's errant ways.

"Your mum's right, Tammy. This isn't your fault. Look, we don't even know if Victor's gambling is the cause of the problem. It's purely conjecture at this time. The last thing you should be doing right now is getting stressed, for the baby's sake," Katy said.

Lorne tilted her head and studied her partner. What she was saying was totally out of character for Katy. *What's going on with you, missy?*" Lorne had an inkling, but she hoped to goodness that she was wrong about it.

Katy caught Lorne eyeing her in puzzlement, and her eyes darted away.

"I know I need to stay calm, but how can I? Victor is dead. My whole world has been ripped apart, and I want to know why. Promise me you'll catch the bastard who has done this."

"You have our word. Will you give us permission to delve into Victor's financial background, look at his bank accounts, *et cetera*? That might throw up some clues for us to follow up on."

"Of course. I have nothing to hide. Neither has he now. As far as I know, he only had the one bank account with Lloyds." She shrugged. "He could have had others I didn't know about, though."

"We have his wallet at the mortuary. We can check how many credit cards he had and get the information we need from them. Is there anything else you can think of that we should know about?"

"Such as what? Isn't that enough?"

"What about his vehicle? Did he have a loan or a lease on that? Again, if he has, that might have been at a higher rate than normal. We could trace it back to the people he was in debt to. Just a suggestion, nothing concrete again. Speculation really."

"The van belongs to work. Our car is in the garage. We can't afford to pay the bill they've given us. It's over five hundred pounds. More stress that we've both had to deal with lately."

"Nonsense. I'll pay that bill for you. You can't be without a car, love. Again, you should have told me that," Eleanor mildly chastised her daughter.

"I can't come running to you with every bill we get, Mum. You have your own expenses to find every month."

"I also have a good pension, too, sweetheart. Anyway, we can discuss that once the detectives have gone. Was there anything else, ladies?"

Lorne and Katy stood up to leave. "If you can just get us the up-to-date bank statements—perhaps mortgage payments, too—we'll be on our way."

Tammy left the kitchen. Moments later, Lorne heard her rummaging through a cabinet and cussing in the next room.

"You will do your best to find the culprit, won't you?" Eleanor pleaded in a hushed voice.

"We will. If Tammy thinks of anything else once we've gone, will you get her to call us? Here's my card. Again, we're sorry to have brought such sad news today. You have our assurances that we won't let this case drop until we find the murderer or murderers."

"Thank you." Eleanor placed the business card on the table. "I'm grateful for anything you do or are able to find out. Knowing that this person is still out there will be playing on our minds. Can you offer Tammy some protection?"

"I can certainly look into the possibility once we get back to the station. I haven't heard anything that would suggest Tammy herself is in any imminent danger, though," Katy replied.

"I can see if she and the kids will come back to my house, but if anything untoward happened to us there, Tammy would never forgive herself. If I can persuade her, and I give you my address, could you see to it that a police car checks our area regularly? That would ease the stress a little."

"I'll arrange that immediately. Tammy really shouldn't be alone right now, so that's a great idea if she stays with you. Ring me at all if you need anything, okay?"

"You're very kind."

After Tammy supplied them with the paperwork they'd requested, Lorne and Katy left the house and headed back to the station.

CHAPTER SIX

The team had their heads down when they arrived back at the incident room. AJ looked up and motioned for Katy to join him at his desk. Lorne hung back, thinking he was going to discuss something personal with her.

Katy turned to face Lorne, wearing a puzzled look.

"Something wrong?" Lorne asked.

"I've been summoned to see the chief."

"Oh, no need to look so worried. I'm sure he just wants a quick update on the case," Lorne tried to reassure Katy, without much success, judging by the way Katy's shoulders slumped and her head hung low as she left the room.

Lorne drew the team's attention, and together, they filled in the incident board with the little they knew about the two victims. "So, should we be looking at the fact that they're both tradesmen as the prime clue here?" Lorne asked.

"It would appear that way," AJ agreed. Then, looking thoughtful, he added, "I don't suppose we should discount the fact that Victor had some kind of gambling problem, either, although nothing has shown up in Paul Lee's accounts to attest to his involvement in the same fate."

"That's true enough. It's clear we need to dig deeper into both men's pasts to see what other similarities they share. I also think we should start delving into their work schedules. I need to know if Victor was at work when he was killed. We're already assuming that Paul was working somewhere on the side. How do we find out where they were working, if indeed that is the link here?"

AJ nodded. "I can see where you're coming from on that, Lorne. Maybe the two firms worked alongside each other occasionally. I'll ring the men in charge, see what they have to say about things. Not sure they'll be able to put us on the right track if they were working on the black, however."

The room fell silent when Katy returned to the room, looking pale. She dropped her backside onto the nearest desk, and Lorne rushed to her side. "Katy? Whatever is the matter?"

"I have to go."

Lorne glanced sideways and saw a concerned AJ approaching. "Katy?" he asked and wrapped a gentle arm around her shoulders.

"It's my Dad. I have to go."

Lorne rubbed her partner's arm. "Oh, no. What's wrong? Is he ill?"

"He's in hospital. Dad's had a heart attack. I don't know if I'm going to make it in time," Katy mumbled as tears slipped from her eyes.

"Go. What are you still doing here? Do you want to take AJ with you?"

AJ looked shocked. "Can I? Should I go with you, Katy?"

Katy shook her head. "No. You stay here. I have to go alone."

Before she could say anything else, the incident room door opened and DCI Sean Roberts entered. "Are you still here, Inspector? I thought I told you to get on the road immediately."

"I'm just coming to terms with things first, sir." She catapulted herself off the desk and ran into her office.

While Katy gathered her things together, Sean called the rest of the team around. "Right, listen up, ladies and gents. DI Foster has an emergency situation she needs to attend to back in Manchester. For the interim, I'm putting Lorne in charge of the case. Actually, we'll be running the investigation jointly, if that's agreeable with you, DS Warner?"

Lorne's eyes almost popped out of her head. *Crap! What do you expect me to do, Sean? Refuse? Nothing like running it by me first and seeing if I'm up to the task before dropping it in my lap like this!* "Of course, why wouldn't I agree?"

Sean grinned smugly. "That's what I hoped you would say. AJ, go and check how Katy is, will you?"

AJ looked as shell-shocked by the unfolding events as Lorne felt. Once AJ was out of earshot, Lorne leaned in to Sean and asked, "It doesn't sound too good for Katy's dad. When did it happen?"

"I got the call while you were out this morning. Her mother didn't want me to contact Katy until she had more news. She didn't want Katy driving all the way up there if it was a mild attack. Apparently, this is his second one in as many years."

"Damn, Katy never said." Lorne stared in the direction of Katy's office. She could hear Katy crying and AJ trying to comfort her.

"The other one was minor compared to this, I think, Lorne. The quicker she gets on the road, the better."

"What about AJ going with her? It's not good for her to be going all that way on her own. I know I wouldn't want to do it."

Sean contemplated the suggestion for a second or two then shook his head. "To be honest, I just don't think we can spare him at this time. I know how callous that sounds, but then I suppose that's the downside of getting involved with someone working on the same team as yourself. I'm sure AJ will understand that the case should, and has to, come first."

"Yeah, he'll understand. I can't see either of them liking the situation, though. Can we not draft someone in from another team for a few days?"

"Limited funds, Lorne. You know the mantra as well as I do. That's the end of the matter as far as I'm concerned. Now, do you think we'll be able to work together well on this case or not?"

Lorne grimaced. *Like I have a lot of choice!* "I'm sure we'll be able to cope... if you can stay out of my way long enough for me to investigate the crimes we've been dealing with."

"Still as spiky as ever, Lorne. So, to go with your role, you better have this new title, Acting Detective Inspector Warner. How's that?"

"Sounds kind of suffocating even to my ears. I'll stick to DS Warner if it's all the same to you," she responded, unimpressed by her newly acquired promotion. All she could think about was how annoyed Tony was likely to be about her temporary role once she informed him. Even though Roberts had twisted her arm, Lorne had gone against the promise she'd made to Tony about not getting too involved when she returned to the Met. She hated the thought of him thinking she was a liar and that, a few years down the line, she would discard the promise as if it meant nothing in the grand scheme of things. This wasn't of her choosing—none of it was. *He'll understand that, won't he?* She asked herself, then cursing her insecurity. She was being totally unreasonable, letting her mind continue to dwell on how her ex-husband—not her present husband—would deal with the scenario. Lorne realised Tony and Tom were akin to yin and yang in that respect.

You're worrying unnecessarily, Lorne.

Katy and AJ came out of the office, neither of them looking as if their time alone had helped.

"Are you sure you're going to be able to drive all that way by yourself, Katy?" Lorne asked, rubbing her partner's arm again.

"Unless the Met wants to let me highjack one of their choppers, I have limited options open to me. It's only a couple of hours, Lorne. I can remain focused for that long I'm sure."

Lorne nodded. "Keep us informed on how your dad is, all right?"

"I will. It'll be via AJ, if that's all right. I want to devote as much time to being with Dad as I can while I'm there. Crap, the guilt is rife right now. Does that ever ease?"

"With time. You have nothing to feel guilty about, Katy. Just go. You should get there before it gets dark."

"I'm going." She turned to AJ and pecked him on the cheek. "I'll call you when I get there, and yes, I'll drive carefully."

The team wished their boss well then returned to work once Katy had left the room. Lorne was aware that she would need to keep AJ busy so his mind wouldn't wander too much. "AJ, I want you to contact both men's places of work to get their itinerary for the last few days. Let's see if we can see any similarities there first before we go down any other lines of enquiries. They might have met up on a previous job or something."

Sean held his hands up in front of him. "Right, I see you have this under control for now, Lorne. I have a few tasks awaiting my attention on my desk. I should be finished within an hour or two."

"You can leave the investigation in our capable hands for now, Chief. I'll call you if I need any assistance."

Sean raised an eyebrow, shrugged, and walked out of the room.

During the rest of the afternoon, the team embarked on their duties in a subdued atmosphere. Lorne found herself distracted when her mind drifted to what Katy was going through. Losing her own father suddenly had been a devastating ordeal for Lorne, one that she wouldn't wish on her worst enemy. She hoped that Katy's father had a strong heart and that he overcame his plight quickly. The statistics of people suffering a heart attack the second they gave up work to enjoy their retirement had never sat comfortably with Lorne. The body was an undiscovered law unto itself at times. She made a note to say an extra prayer for Katy's dad that night.

Mentally exhausted, Lorne instructed the team to call it a day at six. Wearily, she drove home, running through how she should broach the subject to Tony about her forced temporary promotion.

Charlie was in the paddock, training Sheba on the obstacle course, when Lorne pulled into the drive. "Hey, you two, you're looking good. Can you give me five minutes to have a private chat with Tony, sweetheart?"

Charlie waved her hand in front of her. "Of course. We'll be in for dinner in about half an hour, Mum."

"Crikey, give me a chance."

"The dinner is done. No need for you to get your hands dirty. Tony and I threw a few ingredients into a dish and made a chicken casserole."

Lorne blew her daughter a kiss. "You two are brilliant. What would I ever do without you?"

"Mainly? You'd starve. Did you have a good day?"

"I'll fill you in over dinner, sweetie. Quite eventful really," Lorne called over her shoulder as she crossed the driveway and walked towards the house.

Tony was chopping the accompanying vegetables and putting them in a pot when she walked through the back door. "Hello, you. Good day?" He kissed her on the cheek.

"Kind of. Can we sit down and have a chat?"

Tony's nose wrinkled. "Oops... that sounds ominous. Did I do something wrong?"

"Not at all. I think *I* might have, though. Be gentle with me, okay?"

Lorne grabbed Tony's hand and led him over to the table. Once seated, she gripped both of his hands in her own and looked down at the way his fingers entwined effortlessly around hers. She loved this man so much.

"You're starting to worry me, love. Should I be worried?"

"Not really. Okay, I'm just going to come straight out with it. Katy has had to return to Manchester. Her dad's suffered a massive heart attack."

"Oh, Lorne, that's dreadful. What are the odds on him making it?"

"They're not sure yet. She's driven up there alone. It's a tough call for her. She'll ring when she has any news either way."

"I wish her dad the best. Now what are you fretting about? I have a rough idea what you're going to say next anyway."

"You do?"

Tony smiled. "I'm not daft, Lorne. I know how these things work. I take it you're in charge of the team, temporarily, am I right?"

"Yes, you are. Sorry, darling, I tried to get out of it, but..."

"Why are you apologising?"

"Because it means that I will be reneging on a deal we made. That doesn't sit comfortably with me. You'd feel the same if the tables were turned, yes?"

"It's not the same in the slightest, Lorne. This is an emergency. Neither of us could have anticipated such dire circumstances falling upon us. Anyway, I'm not that much of an ogre that I would expect you to keep to your word all the time. 'Shit happens,' as a wise man once said." He leaned forward and kissed the tip of her nose.

"I was so lucky the day you walked into my life."

Tony tilted his head back and laughed. "I seem to recall at the time you were cursing that particular event. We hardly hit it off the second we met, did we?"

Lorne's memory drifted back to the secretive meeting he'd called when he was a MI6 agent, regarding the Unicorn and the mole he'd helped uncover in her team at the time. Actually, Tony had done so much more than uncovering the mole. If it hadn't been for his relentless digging, she would have been none the wiser about AJ coming from a well-to-do family with a father high up in the government. Not that it affected AJ in the least—he was such an unpretentious, compassionate guy. That's why Katy had fallen for him after working alongside him for only a few months.

"Penny for them?"

Lorne shook herself out of her daze. "Just reflecting on our first meeting. That and other similar episodes that have occurred in the years since that eventful day. Like I've said already, I'm lucky to have found you. How's your case going? I take it you've decided to proceed with it?"

"Yep, Joe and I are going to begin in earnest tomorrow. We carried out a few background checks today, just to verify the authenticity of the case, and everything appeared to be genuine enough. We'll start going over the missing man's movements on that day and go from there. I think, initially, it will be a case of pounding the pavement, armed with his photo and asking if anyone can remember seeing him just before he went missing. Let's hope we find the guy anyway. His wedding is fast approaching. I can only imagine the expense that has entailed."

"Good luck. If I can be of assistance, just shout."

"Thanks. I'll tell you what you can do to help right now—either lay the table or dish up dinner."

"I don't mind serving up. I think I'm a little better at portion control than you are. You can go and tell Charlie the coast is clear. I asked her to give us five minutes for a chat."

Tony tutted and shook his head. "You mean you were dreading telling me that much, eh? When will you learn, Mrs. Warner?"

Lorne grinned. "I know. I'm totally dumb at times."

CHAPTER SEVEN

Lorne arrived at work early the following morning to find AJ already tapping at his keyboard. "Did you sleep here last night?"

He glanced up and gave her a quick smile. "Not quite. I worked until ten, went home, and came back in at six this morning."

"Why? Cold bed without Katy around?"

"You know me so well. I miss her."

"I do, too, if it's any consolation. Have you heard from her yet?"

He swivelled his chair in her direction and sat back. "Yeah, her dad isn't so good. Worse than any of them feared, I think. He's on all kinds of machines right now. Not sure he's responding well to the treatment or not. It's hard for them to tell just yet."

"I'm sorry to hear that. Let's try and remain positive about things, eh? What are you working on?"

"I don't know. This and that. A lot of things all at the same time, really. I keep switching between the CCTV discs to the men's background checks, hoping that something I've missed shows up. No good so far, though."

"Don't be so hard on yourself, AJ. You're doing a great job. Whoever said a copper's job was an easy one was a born bloody liar. Nothing is ever cut and dried. You know that, hon."

"I know. I'm just used to spotting things that others fail to see. It's just not working like that on this case. I might dump everything I have and start afresh. What do you think?"

"I still think you're being too harsh on yourself. There is such a thing as trying too hard, AJ—"

The phone on Lorne's desk interrupted her. She took three strides and answered it. "Hello. DS Warner. How may I help?"

"Sorry to disturb you, ma'am. It's control here. I thought you might like to know that a body has been found on your patch."

AJ had turned back to look at his computer screen. Lorne clicked her fingers to get his attention then put the phone on speaker. "I see. And where was the body found?"

"In a car park, close to the river in Wandsworth Park."

"I see. Okay, we'll get down there straight away. I take it the pathologist has been made aware of the discovery and the location?"

"Yes, ma'am. She's on her way down there now."

"Thanks. We'll get over there ASAP, the second the rest of the team turn up for duty."

Lorne hung up. "I suppose I better try and contact the chief, make him aware. I have a feeling I'm going to get lumbered with babysitting him. I'd much rather have you as a partner but... them's the breaks!" She added the last part behind her hand conspiratorially.

"Makes sense to have me here, going through the relevant information, Lorne. Hopefully, something will spring into life soon. I'm still trying to track down one of the bosses of the deceased men to get their worksheet. I'll focus on making that happen while you're out and about today, if you like?"

"Good idea. There has to be something obvious linking these crimes. I'm just hoping this scene doesn't end up being a third victim. The second the controller mentioned the body was found in a car park, the hairs on the back of my neck stood on end."

"Never thought of that. I hope you're wrong."

The door swung open, and the rest of the team filtered in. Lorne filled them in and asked them all to revisit what they'd been working on the day before until any new information came to hand. Then she walked along the corridor to DCI Roberts's office.

His personal assistant welcomed her with a warm smile. "He's just on the phone, Sergeant. Or should that be 'Acting Detective Inspector'?"

"It should be, yes, but you know me—I'm not really one for blowing my own trumpet." She let out a large breath. "Looks like we have another body to contend with. I just hope it's not connected." She looked at her wrist, noting the time—almost nine o'clock. *Come on Sean. Time's marching on.*

"Oh, how awful. There's no such thing as being safe nowadays, is there?" Sean's assistant stated. "Ah, he's finished his call." She leapt out of her chair and knocked on his door. When beckoned, she opened the door and announced Lorne's arrival.

Lorne thanked the woman and walked into Sean's office. "Morning. How's things?"

"Social call is this, Sergeant? And there was me thinking you were knee-deep in a murder investigation."

Lorne pulled a face at him. "I'm just heading out to another scene and wondered if you intended tagging along?"

"I see. Another victim to do with the case you're already working, do you think?"

"My list of attributes might be extensive, but being a mind reader isn't one of them, Chief. I won't know until I attend the scene and see for myself. Are you coming with me, or am I going it alone?"

"Like I told you yesterday, I'll be partnering you on this investigation."

"Then I hate to rush you, but I think we should get our arses over to the scene ASAP."

Sean pushed back his chair and hitched on his jacket. "Then what are we waiting for? My car or yours?"

Lorne shrugged. "Couldn't give a damn, sir."

He winked at her. "I can tell this is going to be fun. Just like old times when we were first starting out on the job."

Lorne turned on her heel, swept her mid-length brown hair over her shoulder, and mumbled, "Christ, I bloody hope not. You were even more insufferable back then."

Patti and her team were already in attendance when Lorne and Sean pulled into the car park. Lorne flashed her ID at the uniformed officer behind the crime scene tape.

"Hi, Patti. I'm not sure if you've had the pleasure of meeting my boss before or not. This is DCI Sean Roberts."

Patti showed her bloody gloves as if apologising for not shaking his hand. "Pleased to meet you. No Katy?"

"No, she's been called away on a family emergency, hence me being lumb… I mean, hence me being partnered with DCI Roberts. Can you tell us if the cases are connected at all, Patti?"

"I've only been here a short time myself, Lorne. However, my initial findings are intimating that might be the case."

"How can you tell, Patti?" Roberts asked as he bent down to study the body.

Lorne tutted and handed him a spare pair of plastic gloves from her jacket pocket. "You might want to put these on, sir, before you go any nearer to the body."

Sean looked up and glared at Lorne. "I'm well aware that I shouldn't touch the body without protection, Sergeant. I'll thank you not to treat me like a novice."

Patti and Lorne exchanged glances. Then Patti pointed out that the body had a head injury similar to the first two victims'. "The only thing different that I've picked up so far is the fact that there was no hosepipe used. That could be a case of the murderers becoming sloppy, or it might indicate the likelihood of them being disturbed around the time the murder was being committed."

"Which is probable, given the location. Why is the murderer carrying out these crimes in such public locations?" Sean asked.

"That's what we're trying to figure out, boss. Why indeed? Have you got an ID on the victim yet, Patti?"

Patti flipped over a wallet she'd already sealed in one of the evidence bags. The man's name and photo stared back at them. "Jeff Whitmore. Here's the thing, you'll never guess what kind of work he does."

"Let me think—judging by what we've found out about the other guys already, I'm going to guess he's a tradesman of sorts. The question is which one?"

"Correct. Looks like he's a plasterer."

"How strange. That has to be the link, doesn't it? Do we know how long he's been dead?" Lorne asked.

Patti chewed the inside of her lip for a second or two. "I'd say no more than four to five hours."

"How do you know he's a plasterer, Patti?" Sean asked. He approached the man's vehicle and looked in the back of the car.

"Well, although the car he's in appears to be a personal vehicle, unlike the other victims, I can see remnants of plaster dust in the rear and a few tools of the trade. Apart from that, his ID states that he belongs to the Master Federation of Plasterers."

Sean rubbed his chin with his thumb and forefinger. "I see. Is he around the same age as the other victims?"

Lorne stood over the victim and assessed his age. "I guess they're similar in age. I'd probably put this guy at being a little older. Why?"

Sean shrugged. "I don't know. Thought it would be a good question to ask."

"Oh, that's all right then. You just let us know if you determine the significance behind your question, boss. Until then, it's always best if we stick to the facts."

Sean glared at her. "Your sarcasm needs to be kept under control, Sergeant."

Patti cleared her throat. "Is playtime finished now, children?"

Lorne chuckled. "Sorry, Patti. I forgot how easy it is to wind my boss up. I promise to behave from now on. So, again, we've established he's a tradesman. We have to be looking at all the men working at the same location, and yet, our initial questioning didn't come up with any likely place of interest."

Sean studied the scene around him, looking thoughtful. "What if their employers didn't know?" he offered.

Lorne rubbed at her chin. "If you're suggesting that each of them were working on the side, we're already looking into that angle."

"Sounds feasible to me."

"What do you think, Patti?"

"I have no idea. All I can give you is the time and cause of deaths on the victims. It's up to you to come up with the whys and wherefores of the case."

"Okay, thinking about it logically for a moment, I think you might be on to something, Sean. The first two victims' bodies were found during the night or early morning. We've yet to determine how long this victim has been lying here. However, considering how early it is now, I think it's safe to presume he was killed around the same time as the other men, yes?"

Patti and Sean both nodded.

"It would appear that way, although I won't be able to verify that until I've carried out the PM," Patti said. "I see where you're going, Lorne. You think the men carried out the work in the evening, long after their normal jobs had been conducted."

"Exactly. It's all adding up to that line of thinking. I've got AJ comparing the first two victims' time sheets to see if they met up on a site somewhere," Lorne said.

Sean shook his head. "Maybe we should do an in-depth study of the areas where the bodies were found and try to draw some kind of conclusion from that. Compare tyre prints to the vehicles, soil debris in the moulds, that kind of thing. How difficult can it be to compare sites?"

"Crap, do you have any idea how many people are renovating their homes or businesses in the London area at present?" Lorne asked.

"I can only imagine," Sean replied.

Patti withdrew from the conversation and carried on with her investigation of the body. "Look, all I can do is search the evidence I have to hand and see if anything significant shows up. Maybe I'll stumble across a receipt or two for supplies that links the victims. Anything right now will be a bonus, won't it?"

"If there's nothing more we can do here, I think we should head back to the station," Lorne said.

Sean frowned. "What about informing the relatives?"

"I meant after we've visited the victim's relatives, of course." Lorne smiled. She'd intended to test Roberts, to see if he could still prioritise what needed to be actioned out in the field. He'd passed with flying colours.

He glanced at her through narrowed eyes. Lorne jotted down the man's address in her notebook then said cheerio to Patti, telling her they'd be in touch later to see if she had any news for them.

"I know what that was about back there," Sean said, inserting the key in the ignition and starting the car.

Lorne placed her hand over her chest and fluttered her eyelashes at him. "Not sure what you're getting at, sir."

"Hmm… oh, look, there's one of those pink farm animals shooting across the sky."

Lorne grinned. "Nice to see you're on the ball anyway. Right, how do I work this complicated contraption?"

"It's a sat nav like any other, Sergeant. Just punch in the address… here, let me do it. First, I have to think about how to proceed in the case, then I have to plan the route, too. Whatever do you do when I'm not around, Lorne?"

Lorne shook her head and puffed out her cheeks. *You walked into that one, girl.* "I leave most things for Katy to do. I generally tend to just tag along for the ride," she told him, glancing out the window as they set off.

"That much I've already figured out for myself, Sergeant. Maybe we should investigate your role with a bit more depth at your next assessment. Agreed?"

Lorne snapped her head round to face him, her mouth hanging open. She was ready to give him a tirade of abuse until she realised it was his turn to wind her up. Instead, she tutted and tapped her wrist. "We should get a move on. The first few hours to any investigation are imperative."

"I'm well aware of the gravity of the situation, Sergeant."

The rest of the journey was conducted in silence. Then as Sean pulled up outside a small terraced house, in a narrow road on the outskirts of Putney, he said, "I'll let you take the lead on this, Lorne."

"Thanks. I'm probably a little rusty myself. Since working with Katy, I've tended to take a backseat on this type of thing."

They left the car and walked up the tiny path to the red front door, which looked newly painted. The road was fairly quiet. Not even a curtain twitched as far as Lorne could tell. She inhaled a large breath and rang the doorbell. A smartly dressed woman in her early forties opened the door.

"Hello. I'm in a rush, so I'd appreciate you being quick."

"Sorry. Are you Mrs. Whitmore?"

Puzzled, she looked both Lorne and Sean up and down. "Yes, and you are?"

Lorne flashed her warrant card in front of the woman. "Acting DI Lorne Warner, and this is my boss, DCI Sean Roberts. Do you mind if we come in for a chat, Mrs. Whitmore?"

The woman seemed confused. "What? Why? The thing is, I have to go out now. If I don't leave within a few minutes, I'll be late for my interview. I need this job, detectives. I can't be late. Can this not wait until later?"

Lorne tried to put the woman at ease with one of her smiles. "I'm sorry. It really is very important."

The woman threw open the front door, turned, and walked back into the house. Once they had joined her in the living room, which was nicely furnished in muted brown tones, Lorne cleared her throat and asked the woman to take a seat.

Sensing that she'd misread the situation, the woman sank into the sofa and clutched her shaking hands together. "Now you're beginning to worry me. Please tell me why you're here."

"Well, it's with regret that I have to inform you that your husband's body was found this morning."

The woman's hand covered her mouth for an instant, then she found her voice again. "You said *body*. What do you mean by that? Just to clarify something, my husband and I are currently separated."

"I'm sorry to hear that. We're treating your husband's death as suspicious."

"Death? How? My God, Jeff is dead!"

"Have you been separated long, Mrs. Whitmore?"

"About a month. He works long hours, *very* long hours, and our relationship has suffered because of that." Her eyes misted up as she clarified things for them.

"Hence you having to find a job, I gather?" Lorne asked.

"Yes. Good heavens, what am I going to do now? If I don't turn up for the interview, they'll think I'm not interested. If I do turn up and people find out I went for the job after you giving me this devastating news, I'll be deemed as heartless. I'm between a rock and a hard place. My Lord, should I even be thinking about getting a job at a time such as this? My God, I'm so confused. Poor Jeff. Poor, poor Jeff."

"I can understand your confusion, Mrs. Whitmore, and I appreciate you talking to us. I have to ask if you knew where your husband was working last night?"

She shook her head, and her gaze drifted off to the left, to the wedding photo on the oak sideboard. The picture was taken on a white sandy beach. Mrs. Whitmore was dressed in a stunning white off-the-shoulder wedding dress, while her husband wore a black tuxedo. "We got married in the Caribbean. Forty of us flew out there. It was one of the best days of my life."

"When did the wedding take place?" Lorne asked.

"Ten years ago," she replied, sadness emanating from her voice. "We were so in love back then."

"What happened? Sorry if that sounds too personal. I'm just trying to build a picture of your husband."

"The hours, his overtime hours. I just couldn't take it anymore. I've been a housewife for years now. At first, I loved being at home, but then he was leaving me alone in the house longer and longer each day. Yes, I know how selfish I sound, especially as he was only working the long hours to make our lives easier. The thing is, the loneliness eats away at you in time. Nothing is really worth being left alone to stare at the walls for thirteen to fourteen hours a day."

"What about the weekends? Did he have time off then?"

"No. After years of putting up with the solitude, I'd eventually had enough. We agreed to separate, but he cut my money off, forcing me to go out and find a job of my own. I don't blame him for his callous behaviour—I'd do the same if I were in his shoes. Now you're telling me he's dead. Was it some kind of accident at work? I said he should rest from time to time. It's not good working all the hours he does. His concentration is bound to slip now and then."

"No. it looks like your husband was murdered, though that's yet to be confirmed by the pathologist."

"Why? Who would kill Jeff? He's hardworking, mate to all and sundry, and never really has a bad word to say about anyone. Why on earth would someone kill him?"

"That's what we're trying to find out. It looks like we have a few other deaths in the area that could be linked. We're just trying to find the connection between the three victims."

"Three victims?"

"Yes. All the victims were tradesmen, like your husband. The first victim was an electrician, the second a plumber, and then your husband was found this morning. He's a plasterer, right?"

"Yes. One of the best in the area. He's never short on jobs because he takes pride in his work."

"Do you know where he has been working recently?"

"Not really. I know he was working on the side, if that's what you're insinuating. His boss didn't know, so I wouldn't bother asking him, either."

"That was going to be my next question—whether his boss was aware of his work on the side. Okay, then my next logical question is, did your husband know either Paul Lee or Victor Caprini? Did he ever mention either man's name?"

Mrs. Whitmore searched her mind but ended up shaking her head in response. "He might have known them, but I can't seem to recall their names. Why?"

"They're the names of the other victims. Are you sure your husband hasn't hinted at the work he's been doing lately? You know, something along the lines of it's an old house that has been gutted by the owners?"

"No. I'd tell you if I thought it would help, I swear."

"Does your husband have a close friend he confides in? Goes out drinking with?" Lorne glanced over at the wedding photo, hoping to see a best man in the picture. There wasn't one.

"No. he never had any spare time, Inspector. His work was his life. He very rarely had any downtime." She nodded at the photo. "That was the last holiday we had. He worked seven days a week, fifty-two weeks a year."

"I see. The only other line of enquiry we're following at the moment is, one of the men had gambling debts of sorts. Can you tell me if Jeff ever gambled?"

She frowned as she thought, then she finally shook her head. "Only on the Grand National, nothing more than that really. Mainly because he didn't have the time to place any bets."

"What about cards? Did he play cards at all?"

"No," she replied more adamantly.

Lorne glanced at Sean, who shrugged in response.

Lorne stood up to leave. "Again, I'm sorry for your loss. We better get back to the station now and begin the investigation in earnest into your husband's death. Will you be all right?"

"I'm not sure. I suppose I'm still in shock."

Mrs. Whitmore showed Lorne and Sean back through the house to the front door, where she bid them farewell and closed the door behind them.

"What now?" Sean asked as they returned to the car.

Lorne threw her arms out to the side and let them slap against her thighs. "Get back to the station. I'm at a loss what to do next on this one. Three murders in, and we're no nearer resolving the case than we were after the first death. What are we missing, Sean?"

"We'll do some brainstorming when we get back over a coffee or two. You're not alone on this one, Lorne. Don't go thinking you have to punish yourself for not solving the case by yourself, okay?"

CHAPTER EIGHT

Tony and Joe began their investigation into Alec Edmond's disappearance, by going through the list of people who'd attended the man's stag party the night he went missing.

"This should be quite easy, as all the partygoers worked at the same factory." Joe ran his finger down the list as Tony drove through the gates of the metal foundry works.

"It'll only be easy if the boss gives us permission to speak to the men while they're at work. If not, we could be in for a long night."

Fortunately, once Tony explained who they were and what they were trying to achieve, Mr. Powell, the managing director of the factory, was only too willing to open up one of the spare offices so they could carry out the interviews there. He even insisted on putting himself forward to be the first in line.

"That's terrific. Thanks," Tony said, relieved.

Tony and Joe sat on one side of the desk, notebooks to hand, while Mr. Powell sat down opposite them.

"Can you tell us in your own words what happened that night, Mr. Powell?" Tony asked.

"Please, it's Ian. Well, we had all arranged to meet up at the Swan just up the road from here at seven."

"This was on Friday of last week, yes?" Joe was quick to ask.

"That's right. We generally work a five-day week, six days when we have a crucial deadline to meet for one of our suppliers. It's pretty slow right now. I specifically asked Alec to consider having the stag do on a Friday. Less likely to have numerous calls saying people are too ill to work the next day that way. Anyway, by seven thirty, everyone who was due to show up had arrived. We stayed at the pub for another hour and then moved on to Tiffany's Club."

"That's the new lap-dancing club in town, right?" Tony clarified.

"Yes, not our usual hangout, I can assure you, but this was no ordinary night. Our mate was getting hitched, and we wanted to give him a good send-off. Anyway, everyone was enjoying themselves. The girls were gyrating their bits onstage even faster than the beer was flowing. We were all having a great time."

When the man paused, Tony looked up from his notes. "I sense you're about to tell us that something changed not long after that. Am I correct?"

"Yes. Well, two guys in the group, Dave and Sid, got a bit mouthy with some college kids sitting at the next table. One thing led to another, and fists soon started to fly."

"Did the bouncers or security men at the club get involved?"

"Did they ever! Their punches turned out to be far harder than the other guys'."

"What happened next? Did you get kicked out?" Tony asked.

"Yeah, the whole lot of us, plus the kids who started the ruckus in the first place. We sobered up pretty quickly once the night air hit us outside. We milled around the town for a while, singing and generally enjoying ourselves, until the small hours of the morning. Then the group dispersed, and we all went home."

"Did you see much of Alec during the night?"

"Yep, he was the centre of attention at all times. We called in at an off licence and bought bottles of cider, vodka, and wine. Took it in turns to hand the bottles around, played a few games, and then went home when we'd had enough."

"So what happened to Alec? Who saw him home?"

Ian Powell shrugged and looked down at his clenched hands on the table. "I'm not sure, is the answer. I looked around for him and presumed he'd departed in one of the first cabs we stumbled across—I really wasn't paying that much attention. It wasn't until we all arrived at work on Monday that we heard he hadn't returned home that night. We've all done our share. Once the guys have finished their shifts, they've all gone straight back out there to search for him. It was my suggestion to call you guys in—well, some form of PI anyway. The police just refused point-blank to investigate his disappearance; said it occurred all the time when men were due to get wed, not that I've heard of that many cases over the years."

"To be honest, that's our experience, too. I have to ask this—is there any way Alec would have gone off with another woman that night? Did he have a former girlfriend still on the scene, for instance?"

Ian shook his head. "Nope, he's devoted to Beth. He'd never let her down, ever. Although saying that, just recently, Marissa has been pestering him at work over the last month or so."

"Marissa? A former girlfriend? Does she work here?" Tony fired off the questions one after the other.

"Marissa Gormon. Alec went out with her for a couple of years, very possessive kind of girl. She heard that he was getting married to Beth and sort of went off the rails. She doesn't work here, but over the last few weeks, she's been showing up to see him, pestering him. I warned him to get rid of her once and for all. He told me that he'd tried, but she wasn't prepared to let things drop. She'd become infatuated with him all over again, he told me. He was distraught about her hanging around here after work. He used to stay later at his station just to avoid being confronted by the bitch outside the gates."

"I don't suppose you have an address for this woman?"

"I haven't, but I'm sure one of the other guys will be able to supply you with one. I definitely think someone should look her up and question her."

"We'll do just that. It does seem suspicious behaviour. Did you see her at any point during the course of Friday night?"

Powell's mouth twisted as he thought. "Can't say I did, but I was more than a tad drunk. Right, that's all I can tell you about what went on that night, chaps. Do you want me to start sending the rest of the staff in to see you?"

"That would be great. Let's hope the others can shed some light on this Marissa woman. It would be good to gather more background information about their failed relationship. Maybe once the stag night came around, the reality of the situation hit home to her, and she tried her hardest to put a stop to the wedding. Pure conjecture of course at this point, but her behaviour does sound as though it belongs in the stalkerish realms to me," Tony admitted.

Mr. Powell left the room and showed the next man in. Fred Elmleigh was a rotund little man who came across as nice enough, if a little quiet. Tony struggled to believe the man had even gone out on the stag night with the other men. *Unless his quiet demeanour is hiding something?*

"No need to be nervous, Fred. We're just trying to figure out what went on that night. Have you heard from Alec since last Friday?"

"No, nothing at all. Not that we were that close, really. I think the guys only asked me to join them because they felt sorry for me. They didn't want me to feel left out."

"I see. So you don't usually go out with the group then?"

"No. Never. I wish I hadn't bothered this time, either. It's shocking what's gone on."

"Did you see Alec get in a taxi at the end of the night, Fred?"

The man shook his head and avoided eye contact with Tony in reply.

Tony had a feeling they were unlikely to get anything useful out of the man and rushed his interview through to its conclusion. "Well, thanks for your help. Can you send the next person in on your way out?"

"Is that it?" Fred looked shocked at being dismissed so early.

Tony tilted his head. "Unless you can tell us anything more of interest, yes. We have quite a few other men to interview and only a couple of hours to do that in. Thanks, Fred."

Disgruntled, the man stood and tucked his chair neatly under the desk before he left the room.

Joe leaned sideways and said in a low voice, "Funny reaction."

"Let's face it—he seemed a 'funny' kind of guy. Let's not dwell on it. He came across as harmless enough."

"If you say so," Joe replied as the next interviewee joined them.

"Hi, I'm Seb. You wanted to have a word with me about Alec?"

"That's right. Take a seat, Seb. Can you run through the events of last Friday for us? We're trying to piece together Alec's last-known whereabouts."

"Sure." Seb told the same story the other partygoers had already told Tony and Joe, adding nothing of any value.

Tony was beginning to think they were merely wasting time going over old ground constantly. That side of PI work didn't really sit comfortably with him. He'd rather have been out there searching for the man the old-fashioned way than being forced to listen to the same words over and over again, like some kind of torture technique.

Another hour passed before they had interviewed all the men who attended Alec's stag night. Frustrated, they left the factory none the wiser and made their way back to the car.

Tony placed his forearms on the roof of the car and let out a long sigh. "What a waste of time that was. Any suggestions what we do next?"

Joe unlocked the doors, and they both climbed into the vehicle. "Well, we do have that Marissa's address now. Maybe we should consider paying her a visit? What do you say?"

Tony nodded. "With very few other options available to us, I say we should give it a shot."

* * *

The address turned out to be a high-rise flat in a block on the outskirts of the city.

"Nice area," Joe mumbled sarcastically.

Disappointed to see the lift out of action, they climbed the stairs to the twentieth floor, passing areas littered with defecation that the council obviously had no intention of cleaning up. The smell of urine clung to Tony's nostrils during the ascent, and he suspected it had also wormed its way into the fine fibres of his suit and would prove near impossible to shift once they got home. At regular intervals, they passed by skinny dogs tied up on the concrete balconies. Tony cringed at the thought of Lorne ever seeing dogs treated like that. She would have let the owners know in no uncertain terms what she thought of them. He dipped his hand in his pocket and threw each of them a couple of chews, which he kept there for emergencies, just in case he needed to distract a guard dog. The dogs pounced on the meaty chews, devoured them, and raised their paws, begging for more.

Joe yanked on his forearm. "Come on, Tony. It's not our responsibility, mate. You're lucky a scrap didn't break out."

"All right. It's not in me to see any creature go hungry."

"Here we are." Joe rapped his knuckles on the door of the flat's filthy door then wiped his hand down the thigh of his trousers.

The door opened to reveal a woman in her late twenties with tousled blonde hair, smudged mascara, and remnants of fluorescent blue shadow around her eyes. She placed her hand over her eyes to block out the sun's rays. "Yeah, what do ya want?"

"Marissa Gormon?" Tony asked.

"Who wants to know?"

"Do you mind if we come in for a few minutes?"

"Yes, I bloody mind. Who the fuck are you?"

"Sorry. I'm Tony Warner, and this is my partner, Joe. We're private investigators."

"Yeah, and? What are you investigating?" she asked, her lip curling up at the side.

Tony heaved a sigh. "If you'll let us in, we'll tell you."

"No way, shitheads. No one comes in my flat uninvited. Say what you've got to say and then get out of my frigging face."

"Okay, if that's the way you want to play it. We're investigating the disappearance of a former acquaintance of yours."

She scratched her head with her scarlet-painted fingernail. "Acquaintance? Who?"

"Alec Edmonds, or should I have said your former boyfriend?" Tony asked.

"Call him what you like. He's a total waste of space." Her eyelids fluttered shut then flashed open again.

"Oh? That's not the impression we got from his colleagues."

"I couldn't give a shit what they've told you. That bitch is welcome to him."

"So, are you telling me that you haven't contacted him in the last few weeks?"

Her feet shuffled, and she pulled her silky robe around her slightly bulging tummy. "I might have."

"Can we ask why?"

"You can ask, but it don't mean to say that I'm going to tell you. That's my business."

"Well, the fact is that our client, Alec's fiancée, has employed us to look for him. So any recent involvement you've had with him automatically becomes our business."

"That's bullshit. Even if you were the boys in blue, I still wouldn't talk to you about what went on between us. It's *our* business. Got that?"

"I hear you, Ms. Gormon. There really isn't any reason for you to shout at us like that. Have you seen him recently?"

"Nope."

"You do know it's an offence to withhold evidence in someone's disappearance?" Tony bluffed.

The woman laughed in his face. "Bullshit. Now, if you don't mind, I need to get back to my beauty sleep."

Tony stifled the grin that was keen to escape. *You'd need several years of non-stop sleep to obtain that, dear lady.*

"Thanks for your time. We'll be passing our findings over to the police investigation team soon, so expect a visit from them in the near future."

"That's another dose of bullshit, man, and you damn well know it. Never bullshit a bullshitter. Hasn't anyone told you that before?"

Tony was about to hit her with a sarcastic retort about meeting plenty of bullshitters over the years in his role as a MI6 operative, but she slammed the door in his face.

"Nice lady." Joe chuckled.

"Yeah, I suppose she feels well at home living in a dump like this. Nice lady, nice area, nice life. Come on. Let's go back to the scene and see what we can find. We've wasted enough time around here as it is."

CHAPTER NINE

The team gathered around, then armed with cups of steaming coffee, they thrashed out the relative facts to the cases. Lorne studied each of the team members, as one by one they revealed their conclusions. Nothing significant jumped out until AJ stepped forward and tapped the incident board with his pen.

"The only thing grabbing me is how much these cases are going to be dependent on the CCTV footage."

"With nothing else showing up, I think you might be right, AJ," Lorne agreed.

Sean folded his arms and rested his backside on a nearby desk. "Didn't you say at the first scene, the number plate to the other vehicle had been masked in some way?"

Lorne nodded. "That's right, but at least we know what kind of vehicle it is. Don't we, AJ?"

"We do. What if I run the make, colour, *et cetera* through the system, plus the areas where all three bodies were found—they're in pretty close proximity to each other, aren't they? That in itself is a good indicator that the murderers live close by."

"Great idea. Get on that right away, please. Anyone got anything else?"

Karen raised her hand. "If the men were working on the black, perhaps they dropped some kind of hint about the work they were undertaking to their workmates. It might be worth having a chat with them, boss."

"Agreed," Sean said, smiling at Karen.

"Stephen and Graham, I'd like you to arrange with each of the companies to quickly interview their staff, see if anything shows up there."

Both men nodded, then Stephen suggested another good idea. "Shall I ask the bosses at each of the firms if they keep a record on mileage?"

Lorne tilted her head. "What are you getting at, Stephen?"

"Well, I'm not sure how relevant it will prove to be regarding the third victim, but the first two vics were found using their companies' vehicles, weren't they? Perhaps they had to log their mileage with the firms at the end of each working day. Armed with the information from those logs, maybe we'll be able to work out how far the location where they were working on the sly is from their company's headquarters and where their vehicles were dumped."

"I'm with you. It'll help in relation to AJ investigating the vehicle of the murderers, too." Lorne's heartbeat quickened with the prospect of stumbling across something that could lead to the murderers' arrests. "What else do we have? There's no proof of DNA that we know of yet at either of the scenes, and no sign of the weapon that was used to kill the vics, either. Any other suggestions?"

The team shook their heads in unison.

"The only other thing I can suggest is going to the media," Karen offered.

"Hmm… I'm inclined to leave that for a little while, Karen. It might make us look stupid, especially as we have very little evidence to hand right now. Let's revisit that once we've gone through what we've just discussed, okay?" Lorne said.

"Rightio."

"Okay, people, let's dig deep and see what shit we can find."

By the end of the shift, AJ had uncovered three likely cars matching the description of the killers' vehicle. Stephen and Graham returned to tell them that none of the victims' colleagues could shed any light on where the men had been working on the black. That side of things was more exasperating to Lorne than she had anticipated.

Sean Roberts had returned to his own office during the afternoon and had only just reappeared for an update.

"So, if we have three addresses, do you want to check those out in the morning, Lorne?"

"Logically, I think we should do it tonight, just in case another tradesman's life is in danger, not that there are that many left to kill off. Most of the trades—electrician, plumber, plasterer—have already been covered. But realistically, I think we would be better chasing them up in the morning."

"Then that's what we'll do. Let's call it a day here. Good work, folks. Hopefully, things will start looking up for us tomorrow. Good night, all."

Lorne left the station with AJ. "Great work today, AJ, considering the amount of stress you must be under."

"Thanks. I'm eager to remain busy. It's hard blocking Katy and her dad's circumstances out, though. I'm going to ring her later. Thought I'd leave it until about nine. She should be home from the hospital by then. Just wish I could have travelled up there with her."

"I know. It's a tough call. Maybe you should start applying for jobs in other divisions now, in case something like this rears its head in the future, eh?"

"I'm not so sure. It's going to be a major pull leaving this team. The thought of not working alongside Katy is a killer, but worse than that, not being involved in such a shit-hot team, I fear would be detrimental to my career. It's a toss-up to know what to do for the best."

"I know. Look, all I can say is that when I was out of the team, the one thing I missed the most was the camaraderie. You're right—we are a great group of detectives. However, there's one major thing against you—the higher-ups won't put up with you and Katy being an item for long without moving at least one of you to either a different team or force."

"I hear you. I'll mull it over thoroughly this evening. Goodnight, Lorne."

"Give my love to Katy when you talk to her. See you in the morning."

Lorne watched AJ walk over to his sports car, a dejected figure with what looked like the world pressing down heavily on his shoulders. She didn't envy one iota the decision process that lay ahead of him that evening.

The next morning, Lorne spent the first hour going through the pile of post that had miraculously appeared on Katy's desk overnight. A knock on the door around ten came as a welcome relief. She glanced up to see an amused Sean leaning against the door frame.

"I've come to save you."

Lorne pushed away the forms and sat back in her chair. "Have you finished your paperwork yet?"

"Nope. I'll never finish my paperwork. I have left it at a convenient moment, though. We should set off soon."

Lorne stood, slipped on her navy suit jacket, and followed him back out into the incident room. She collected the addresses they were due to visit from AJ. "Okay, we're off. Just keep digging until we return, folks."

"Maybe we should have asked an armed response team to accompany us today," Sean said, he opened his car door then jumped in behind the steering wheel.

"We don't want to seem to be going in there heavy-handed, Sean."

"What kind of deterrent do you have to hand?"

"Pepper spray—that's usually enough to combat any unjust behaviour. I'm up for a Taser session soon. I wonder who put me forward for that?"

Sean grinned. "I know how you've been banging on for years that Met coppers should be armed. Well, this is the next best thing. I thought you'd jump at the chance to have a high-voltage weapon in your hand."

"You certainly have a way with words, Sean. Yes, I think it's the way we should be going, although I'd still be careful whom I used the darn thing on. Even those things can be lethal if used in the wrong circumstances."

"That's why it's important to use them more as a deterrent than an actual weapon. The officers in charge of the Tasers are told to shout and warn offenders before they aim their weapons and fire them. We've only had a few instances where the weapon has been used and the perpetrator has ended up in either the hospital or the mortuary."

"I can still see the Met getting sued by those struck. Let's face it, offenders don't need much to start waving the human rights flag in the face of authority when it suits."

"I have every confidence that you'll use it responsibly, Lorne."

"That, I can guarantee."

They arrived at the first address within twenty minutes of leaving the station. Outside the small terraced house, Lorne pointed at the black Ford Mondeo. "Looks like the person we've called to see is in."

Lorne eyed the car with concern. Even though the image of the vehicle had been super grainy, she still had a suspicion the car wasn't the one they'd spotted on the CCTV cameras. She decided to keep this information to herself for the time being. Surveying the outside of the property, she had serious doubts that any form of renovation work had happened at the house in the past thirty years, let alone the last few weeks.

Armed with her warrant card, she knocked on the front door. They waited and waited for the door to open. In the end, Sean clenched his fist and banged heavily on the door five times.

"All right, all right. I'm comin'." The door opened and a swaying man in his mid-twenties, wearing a food-stained T-shirt and striped boxer shorts, hung on to the door jamb for support.

Lorne got the impression he was either extremely hungover or very high on drugs. She flashed her ID in front of his dazed face. "Acting Detective Inspector Lorne Warner and DCI Sean Roberts. Mr. Tennant?"

"Yeah. What do you lot want?"

"One question—actually two, if you don't mind. Does the Mondeo belong to you?" Lorne jerked her thumb at the car.

"Yeah, and?"

"Mind if we come in for a chat?"

"Yes, I do. What's all this shit about?" he asked aggressively, trying to force himself to focus hard on what was going on if the strained expression on his face was anything to go by.

"It would be better to chat inside," Lorne insisted. She took a step towards the man, but he refused to relinquish his hold on the door.

"No."

Sean winked at Lorne. "I'll have to ask you to accompany us to the station in that case, Mr. Tennant."

The man's head tilted first one way then the other. "What? What the fuck for? What have I done wrong?"

"Well, for a start, you're obstructing a police enquiry into a murder case, and for another, it looks like you're high on what I'm guessing to be an illegal substance. Am I right?"

The man's eyes switched between expanding and narrowing, the more irate he grew. "No. On both counts."

Sean barged past Tennant and pulled Lorne by the forearm before the man could object and slam the door in her face.

"Hey, what the fuck? You can't come in here like that."

"If you have nothing to hide, then you won't mind if we take a quick look around, will you?"

The detectives walked farther into the house, which smelt of a mixture of rancid takeaway cartons and the herby, citrusy smell of

Marijuana. Lorne shook her head and pinched her nose in disgust. "I'll take a look upstairs while you chat with him, if you like?"

"Thanks. I get all the peachy jobs."

Lorne grinned and ran up the stairs two at a time. *The quicker we get out of this dump, the better—if only for health reasons.* She swiftly moved between the rooms on the first floor and saw no evidence of any renovation work— just an eyesore of clutter and grime in every room. Every square inch of the property was filled from floor to ceiling with *stuff*—old newspapers and cardboard boxes that seemed as though they were about to burst open, and spill their contents at any second. The one saving factor was that the smell upstairs turned out to be far less intrusive than what she'd left Sean to contend with downstairs.

"Anything, Inspector?" Sean shouted, obviously as eager as she was to withdraw from the premises.

"Nothing, boss. I'm coming now." Lorne started back down the stairs then realised she hadn't looked behind the final door on the landing. Tentatively, she pushed open the door. What it revealed made her stomach lurch, and she almost lost its contents. The bathroom was pure filth. Scum marks were clearly visible in the bathtub. The toilet was virtually full to the brim with toilet paper. *Shit! I dread to think what is lurking beneath that. Nope, I've seen all I need to see in this dump!*

Lorne swiftly descended the stairs. "Have you checked down here?" she asked Roberts. Looking into his eyes, she could tell he was chomping at the bit to leave.

Sean nodded and sighed. "Yep, nothing here."

"What did I tell you? Now, fuck off and leave me alone."

Lorne walked past and glared at the man. "You're filth. You need to get this place cleaned before your neighbours start complaining about the stench. The council has the right to order you to clean this place up if people's lives are at risk, you know. If they aren't living here already, I bet an army of rats will find their way in and take up residence soon."

The man visibly cringed. "You're winding me up?"

"Nope, deadly serious. Get off your lazy friggin' backside, stop smoking dope, and clean this shithole up ASAP."

Sean burst out laughing once they were back in the car. "That's what I love about you—you're such a straight talker."

"I doubt it'll make a difference. He'll consider what I said for all of ten seconds. Jesus, how the hell people live in such hovels is beyond me. I'm going to do him—and the neighbours—a favour and report him. I wasn't joking back there. The rat population is growing in this country because of dunderheads like that, owning properties and not maintaining them properly. I saw a programme about it on TV last week."

Sean laughed again. "It's really incensed you, hasn't it?"

"Too bloody right." She looked over her shoulder at the backseat. "Why don't posh cars like this come with a shower cubicle? They bloody well should."

Sean ignored the comment and put the car into gear. "Where's the next address?"

"Around five miles south of here."

"Let's hope the house is in better nick than this one. Not sure the inside of my nose could take another battering."

"Mine either."

They pulled up outside the address, but there was no sign of the vehicle in the street. "I'll go and knock on the door just in case. You never know—the car might be in the garage or workshop," Lorne volunteered, jumping out of the car.

She knocked on the front door but received no answer. Then she decided to ask the neighbours on either side of the property if they knew much about the occupants. The first neighbour answered the door almost immediately. Lorne flashed her warrant card and introduced herself to the elderly lady cowering behind the door.

"Hello, what can I do for you?"

"Hi, sorry to trouble you. I'm trying to locate your neighbour, Mr. Franks. Is he around?"

"Oh dear, is he in trouble with the police?"

"No. I just want to ask him a few questions. Is he at work?"

"Yes, so is his wife." The woman appeared to relax a little and came out from behind the door.

"I don't suppose you know where the couple work?"

"No, dear. I tend not to mix with many people nowadays. Neighbours come and go all the time. Not worth trying to form a relationship any longer. You understand that, don't you?"

"That's a shame. I completely understand where you are coming from. One last question before I go. Do you know if the property owners have been carrying out any form of renovations on their home recently?"

The woman shook her head. "Not that I know of, dear. At least, I haven't heard anything. Next door on the other side have been fixing up their kitchen. It's been a nightmare for a good few months now. I'm sure I would have heard if the Franks had been doing the same sort of thing. Had to up my intake in painkillers lately due to the headaches I've been getting because of the damn noise."

"Sorry to hear that. I hope they complete their work soon and give you your peace and quiet back. You've been such a big help. Thank you."

"Not at all, dear."

Lorne skipped back to the car. "Looks like we have one more roll of the dice."

"I hope this turns out to be the answer. Not sure what we're going to do if it's another false alarm," Roberts said.

"I guess it's possible AJ might have missed a vehicle off the list. Let's not draw any conclusions yet until we've visited the final house."

CHAPTER TEN

The car drew their eye immediately. "Well, at least the owner appears to be at home this time. We should both go, yes?" Lorne suggested.

Sean parked in the nearest available space, and together, they approached the house, which was in a far better area than the previous two addresses. "This part of Islington is supposed to be under redevelopment plans, isn't it?"

Lorne nodded. She'd heard something along those lines. Anyway, renovations were a totally different prospect from when she had renovated her first house in nearby Highbury, after divorcing Tom—there had been no assistance from the council then. She knocked on the door. A woman in her early fifties greeted them with what could only be described as a cautious smile. "Can I help?"

Lorne showed her ID.

The woman took it and studied it for several seconds before handing it back to Lorne.

"Is it convenient to come in for a chat, Mrs. Platt?"

The woman's eyes narrowed for a flickering instant when Lorne mentioned her name. "About what exactly? I was on my way out."

Sean tried to disarm the woman with one of his most dazzling smiles. "We won't keep you long. It's regarding an important police matter."

Reluctantly, the woman stepped aside to let them in. The Victorian house was immaculately decorated. From the lack of tell-tale cobwebs attached to the original cornicing, Lorne could tell the woman took pride in her home. She closed the front door then opened the door to the large lounge. A man of a similar age to the woman's was sitting in a leather armchair, reading a daily newspaper. "Courtney, this is DS Warner and DCI Roberts. They've come to ask us a few questions."

Lorne didn't correct the woman on her title. Instead, she watched the couple's interaction carefully, but she didn't really pick up on anything out of place. The man folded his newspaper and tucked it down the side of the chair. He stood up and shook each of the detectives' hands. Lorne almost cried out in pain when the man's firm grip squeezed her hand.

"What sort of questions?" he asked.

"I told them that we're just on our way out, love," Mrs. Platt said quickly—too quickly for Lorne's liking.

A note of suspicion rippled up her spine.

"We can spare the nice police folks ten minutes, Cathy. Now, what can we do to help?"

There was something insincere about the smile lingering on Mr. Platt's lips.

"We'd like to know if you've carried out any renovations on your property in the last few weeks?" Lorne asked.

The couple glanced at each other, then shook their heads in unison. "No. Why?"

Sean asked, "So, you won't mind us taking a look around the property then?"

Mr. Platt fidgeted on the spot, but his tight smile never faltered. "If you wish. We have nothing to hide. If you choose not to take our word then, please, go ahead."

Lorne set off. She could hear Sean asking the couple more questions as she made her way up the stairs, which were carpeted with a floral pattern. She pushed open the first door. A double bed filled the room. The place was a stark contrast to the previous house they had visited. Lorne looked down at the carpet, where she could see the lines from the vacuum, which had probably been made that morning. There wasn't a piece of clothing on view. She pulled open the wardrobe to find everything neatly lined up in colour order throughout. Shoes still in boxes were wedged onto the top shelf. Lorne opened the door and peeped inside the next robe to see the same organisation skills had been at work there, too.

The room next door appeared to be a child's bedroom—a single bed, beautifully made up with pink cushions and a Barbie quilt cover, was pushed up against the wall, giving the child plenty of floor space where she could play with her toys. However, the room was empty, except for the bed, a wardrobe, and a small chest of drawers. *That's strange! This place is pristine! Do any kids actually live here?*

Carrying on with her search, Lorne popped her head around the door to the next room. Again, she found nothing out of place. The room's furnishings comprised of a set of bunk beds, with not a crease in sight on either of the two beds. She detected the faint smell of furniture polish. Inquisitiveness got the better of her, and she knelt on the floor and peeked under the bed. Again, nothing. No specks of dust. Nothing. Most kids she knew kept something under their beds. Even she had been guilty of that during her rebellious teenage years. *Perhaps I'm doing them an injustice.* Judging by the couple's age, she thought it possible that the kids had all grown up and flown the nest. Keeping the rooms clean would have been easy if no one used them.

Feeling perplexed, Lorne returned downstairs, where, to her surprise, Sean was laughing and joking with the couple. "I'm good to go when you are, sir," Lorne said.

Sean shook first the man's hand then his wife's. Lorne didn't, not that the couple offered to shake her hand anyway. In the car, Sean said, "Nice couple."

"Hmm..." Lorne murmured, glancing out the window.

"What's that supposed to mean, Sergeant, sorry, Acting Inspector?"

"Just hmm... let's say the jury is still out for me."

Sean chuckled. "Oh crap, I forgot about you working a lot on gut instinct as opposed to usual policing methods."

"It's always seen me good in the past, Sean. Let's see if my gut proves me right on this case, eh?"

"Deal. Back to the station now that we've exhausted everything out here?"

"Whatever." Lorne spent the rest of the journey mulling over the houses they'd visited, and more questions than answers filled her mind about the last property. However, she wasn't prepared to share her concerns with Sean after he'd taken the piss out of her and infuriated her.

As they walked into the station, Sean observed, "You're quiet."

"Thinking, that's all. I tend to do a lot of that form of activity during a case."

"Still full of sarcasm, I see, Lorne."

Climbing the stairs ahead of him, she mumbled, "Better than being full of shit, like some I could mention."

"Did you say something insolent, Sergeant?"

She turned to look at him, wide-eyed, and placed a hand on her breast. "Acting Inspector, actually. *Moi* say something disrespectful? Never."

At the top of the stairs, Sean announced, "I'll leave you to it then and get on with some paperwork. I'll drop by after lunch to see what the team has come up with, okay?"

"Fine." Lorne issued him a taut smile and pushed open the door to the incident room. "We're back. Found out anything while we've been out and about?"

AJ eyed her suspiciously. "Nothing this end, but it looks like you've uncovered something."

"Has anyone ever told you how astute you are, AJ? How can you tell?"

"By the glint in your eye."

Lorne winked at him and pointed her finger. "You understand me better than the chief does. Gather around, people. I want to run a few things past you."

Chairs scraped as the team moved into position. Lorne picked up the marker pen and jotted down the relevant information she and Sean had gleaned from the first two addresses, but she deliberately avoided noting down anything about the third address until she had gained the team's full attention.

"So, it was a waste of time going out to the addresses I gave you then?" AJ asked.

"Not really, AJ. The first address was pointless. The second address, we need to revisit as the homeowner was out, but the neighbour didn't think they had carried out any recent renovations, unlike her neighbour on the other side. We'll still pay the owner a visit, though, just to cross them off the list. However, when we visited the third address—how shall I put this? I suppose the couple sparked more than a little interest in me, but only *me*."

"You're saying the chief didn't share your concerns, boss?" Graham asked, tilting his head and frowning.

"Correct." She looked over her shoulder at the door to check the coast was clear then whispered, "But then we have to make exceptions for him. He's been pushing paper for far too long now." The team laughed. "Anyway, I want proper—by that I mean, thorough—background checks carried out on the Platts. Instinct tells me we're going to find a lot. Whether it will be of any benefit to our case, only time will tell on that one."

"Are we looking for anything in particular, boss?"

"Anything and everything, AJ. Their house was immaculate. No sign of any renovations anywhere. That doesn't mean we're barking up the wrong tree. They could be renovating another house somewhere. Karen, can you look into that side of things, the financial trail, mortgages, rent-to-buy mortgages. That's always a good indicator."

"Okay, sorry to keep mentioning it, but I wondered if we should put out a plea to the media now."

Thinking, Lorne tapped the side of her chin with the marker pen. "Maybe now would be an ideal time to do that. Can I leave it with you to sort that out, Karen? Can you do both tasks?"

"Of course I can. Leave it with me. The media attention could throw up some news of possible vehicles we may have missed."

AJ nodded. "It's worth a try. Would it be better to mention the car *and* the renovations? It might prompt someone into making a connection."

"Great idea. If the Platts are involved and they've bought a place on the side to do up, someone out there might be able to highlight the property for us." Lorne clapped her hands in glee. "I have a positive feeling about this, people. Keep up the good work. There's another thing that concerns me about this couple that I think we should delve into also."

"What's that, boss?" Stephen asked as the other team members got back to work.

"The house was immaculate. Not only that, when I nosed around upstairs, it appeared that the couple had children, but there was no sign of any toys or any kind of mess in either of the bedrooms. It just struck me as being very odd."

Stephen frowned. "Did you ask them if they had kids? What age were the couple?"

"Early fifties, I suppose. No, it was weird—when I came back downstairs, the chief was laughing and joking with the couple. I know I should have interrupted them and asked the question. The thing is, I just wanted to get out of there for some reason ASAP. The chief doesn't go by gut instinct, so there was no point in me trying to justify how I felt in the couple's presence. I just wanted to get back here and start digging. So, let's see if this couple comes up smelling of roses or horseshit."

Karen raised her hand to speak and dropped the phone back in its cradle on her desk. "We're on for tomorrow, boss. I tried to get them to slot it in on tonight's news, but it was too late."

"Excellent. That's still quick, Karen. Thanks for that. Okay, I'll be tackling Katy's mountain of paperwork if anyone needs me." Lorne stopped at the vending machine en route to the office and bought a coffee, then she settled behind Katy's desk to carry out her least favourite chore.

Lorne was only a short way through the pile of letters and files when Karen knocked on the door. She beckoned her colleague in to take a seat.

Karen placed her notebook on the desk in front of her and smiled. "I thought you'd like to know what I've found out right away."

Lorne leaned back in her chair, linked her hands together, and steepled her index fingers against her chin. "Sounds intriguing. Go on."

"I didn't find any evidence of any large sums in either of the Platts' accounts, although I did find notification of a loan they'd taken out in the last few months."

"A loan? For how much?"

"Twenty thousand."

"Interesting. I don't suppose the bank would say what the loan was for?"

Karen shook her head. "No, they wouldn't divulge that information. It certainly looks like a renovation amount to me. If they haven't splurged on a new car recently, which is certainly the case, then what else would they spend that amount of money on?"

"A holiday?" Lorne suggested.

"Nope. I took special note of the activity on their account. The loan was in Mr. Platt's name. Right after the loan was granted, some large amounts started to be withdrawn from the account. The odd thousand here and there."

"Payments for work carried out on the sly? Cash-in-hand payments, is that what you're surmising, Karen?"

"Yep. I studied the statements more and also spotted several purchases the couple had made by cheque to B&Q, too."

"A DIY outlet. Now that is interesting, considering they clearly stated they hadn't done any work on the house lately. The plot thickens. Has Stephen come up with anything about the kids yet?"

"Not yet. I think he's on his fifth call. Keeps getting put on hold and forgotten about, I think. Bloody social services!"

"They're under pressure, just like the rest of us. Okay, let me know when that information is available. Thanks, Karen, great work."

When Karen left the office, Lorne tried to concentrate on the paperwork but failed wretchedly. Her mind spun off in different directions. Most prominent was the fact that the Platts had tried to dupe them. *Sneaky shits! What are they up to? Did they carry out the work at that property or somewhere else?* Lorne had an inkling the truth would turn out to be the latter, but she had no idea where. What were they missing? More to the point—what was *she* missing?

That afternoon, Stephen finally received the news from social services he'd been impatiently waiting for. Lorne came out of her office just as he answered the call. She perched her backside on the desk next to his and listened to the conversation on speakerphone.

"So the couple are foster parents. Okay, and do they have any children of their own?"

Lorne heard paper rustling on the other end of the line before the woman spoke again. "Yes, they have a grown-up son. At the moment, they are fostering three children."

Lorne's eyes grew wide. "Sorry, this is Acting Detective Inspector Lorne Warner here. My colleague has you on speakerphone. Can you tell me what sort of age these children are?"

"Sure, just a second. Here we are. There are two girls. Emily is six, Colette is five, and the little boy, Dwain, is seven. All members of the same family."

"Really? And how long have they lived with the Platts?" Lorne asked.

"For the past three months. They were taken away from their mother."

Lorne frowned at that piece of surprising news. "For what reason?"

"The mother stabbed the father repeatedly. He died at the house. The kids were all traumatised at the scene. They saw the attack."

"That's awful. I'm sorry to hear that. Can I ask why the Platts were considered to be suitable foster parents?"

"I'm not sure I understand what you're getting at? In what respect?"

"Sorry, the Platts seem to be of a certain generation. How would someone of their age be expected to take care of three traumatised youngsters?"

"Are you telling me they're not coping with the situation? Because that's news to me. I only visited them last week, and everything seemed just fine then."

"No. Nothing like that. I just wondered why social services would place three young siblings at a home of an older couple. Wouldn't it be better to place the children with a younger family?"

"It depends. We're under pressure to home the children as soon as they come to us. If a younger family isn't available at the time, then we place them where we can, with reliable families we've worked with in the past."

"I see. So you're telling me the Platts have always been dependable in your eyes?"

"Yes. Seriously, I have no idea why you're questioning this family's trustworthiness."

The woman's voice rose to a shrill, proving how irate she was becoming with Lorne's intrusive questions. Lorne decided to back off just in case the woman considered ringing the Platts to make them aware of the conversation they were having.

"Thank you. I'm only asking because the couple's name has been highlighted in a case we're working on at the moment."

"Do you think our department should be concerned by your investigation?"

"Not yet. To be honest, we have a media plea going out in the next few days. We'll know more after that has aired. I'll get back to you if I believe the children in the couple's care are at risk. One last question, if I may?"

"Go ahead."

"When you visited the house last week, did you hear or see any sign of renovations going on at the house? Or did either of the Platts mention they had purchased another house and were doing it up at all?"

"I don't recall hearing any noise resembling any form of work going on at the house, and as for the second part of the question, why on earth would they bring that sort of information into a conversation with me?"

"It was a long shot, I know. Sorry, I promise this is my final question."

The woman let out a long sigh. "I have to get on."

"Just a quick one. What condition was the house in when you last saw it?"

"I don't understand? I've already said that I didn't see any work in progress at the house."

"Sorry, I didn't make myself very clear. I've just visited the property and found it in immaculate condition. No sign at all that any kids lived there. Was it like that when you visited them?"

"Yes, it's always spotlessly clean. What can I say? Mrs. Platt takes pride in her home. In my experience, that is a rarity. Between you and me, I wish we had a hundred families like the Platts on our books. Sadly, we don't."

"Well, thanks for your time. Our little chat has been most helpful."

"My pleasure," the woman replied before the line went dead.

Lorne exhaled a large breath that puffed out her cheeks. "This couple is becoming more and more questionable to me. Is there some kind of major cover-up going on at their house, or what?"

Stephen shrugged. "I wouldn't like to say at this point, boss. I know when I've visited my mate's house—he has three kids—his house always has that 'lived-in look.' Hey, Graham, when was the last time you saw the colour of your living room carpet?"

Graham's brow furrowed. "What the fu... sorry, boss. What in God's name are you talking about?"

"We're having a discussion about house tidiness when you have kids. Care to share your experience with us, for research purposes, of course?"

"Ah, I see. Well, I regularly go home after a shift and think I've entered a war zone. Actually, that's my first job when I get in—tidy up the living room. Neither Liz nor I can stand watching the TV after the kids have gone to bed with every toy they own surrounding us. I wouldn't have it any other way, though."

"My point exactly. With kids around, there is never any harmony in the living area, and quite often, their bedrooms can be far worse," Stephen added, sounding like a leading authority on the subject.

"Thanks for that insight, Stephen."

The team spent the rest of the day digging into every crevice of the Platts' past, and by the time the end of the shift came around, Lorne's frustration was almost at a tipping point. She drove home, the CD playing extra loud while she tried to flood out the thoughts that kept spiralling like a tornado in her mind. She made a conscious decision to make a detour on the way home and stopped by her good friend Carol's house. After reflecting upon the last spiritual encounter she'd had in her psychic friend's living room, she almost changed her mind and drove straight home. Instead, she plucked up the courage and knocked on the door to Carol's house. Onyx, the rescued boxer dog that Carol had taken a shine to at the kennels, barked until the front door opened.

Lorne squeezed past the enthusiastic dog and attempted to kiss Carol on the cheek, but her friend pulled away. "Don't, I'm full of a million germs. I'd hate for you to pick up what has had me bed-ridden for days. I should be better by Monday, if that's why you've come to see me."

"Don't be silly. You get yourself well first. Charlie can handle the kennels by herself for an extra few days. Tony and I are on hand, helping out where we can, too."

"Oh great, now I feel doubly guilty. You guys have enough to do in your own busy work schedules without carrying out my chores, too."

Lorne waved away Carol's apology. "Nonsense. It's you who's doing us the favour, remember? Have you visited the doctor?"

"Yes, I'm due to have a chest X-ray on Tuesday. I feel tons better. Think it's probably run its course by now, but the doc just wants to make sure."

"Very wise. Look, there's no point coming back to work on Monday if you're not a hundred percent better. Take another few days off."

"If that's okay? I'll come back on Wednesday. Maybe I can work the weekend and give Charlie a break. She could go away for a few days with her friends, perhaps?"

"We'll see. How are you apart from having the flu?"

"So, so… I was going to ring you later about something I've picked up recently."

"Oh, sounds intriguing."

"Well, don't get your hopes up too much. It might not come to much, what with my brain being super fuzzy right now."

"Anything you can give us at this stage would be great, Carol. This is a rather perplexing one."

Carol sniggered. "Aren't they all? Sit down. I'll see what I can do."

They sat opposite each other at the large dining table, and before long, Carol started rocking back and forth as the information came to her from the spirit world. A pained expression twisted her features.

Lorne took out her notebook, ready to jot down anything Carol threw at her.

"My guides are showing me a dark place, stone walls, wet walls. A river, a drunken man, exposed electrical wiring, smoke, some form of pipe—not the smoking variety, before you ask. A heart attack. A hospital. That's all."

Lorne wrote the information down as quickly as it was delivered. "Some of it rings true with the case I'm working at the moment. Damn, I should have told you when I arrived. Katy has returned home to Manchester—it's her dad."

"No. Don't tell me he's the heart attack victim?"

"Yep, I'm afraid so. He's in a critical condition... I don't suppose you can work your magic and tell me what the outcome will be? I promise not to tell Katy."

Carol shook her head and closed her eyes. "No. I can't get past him lying in a hospital bed."

Lorne gasped.

Carol was quick to counter her morbid assumption. "Get that thought out of your head. It doesn't mean the news is bad. It's just that I can't see past his illness at this present time. You, of all people, should know how this works by now, Lorne."

"Phew... that's a relief."

"What about the other things I gave you. Any good?"

"Some I can make use of. Others are pretty obscure but could come to light further on in the case."

"Good. I'm glad I can be of some help again." Carol pointed her finger at Lorne. "Of course, some of those clues could refer to Tony's case, too. You know we sometimes get crossed wires now and again. That's up to you to sift through the relevant details."

"Tony and I will put our heads together over the weekend." Lorne let out a breath. "Boy, am I ready for some time off. It's been a hectic week so far, what with Katy abandoning ship."

Carol tutted. "Lorne! I'm surprised at you, saying such an appalling thing."

"I didn't mean anything by it. Merely stating facts. And to crown it all, I'm now lumbered with Chief Roberts as a partner."

"Ah, now we're getting to the crux of the matter. It's not so much Katy's desertion that's bothering you; it's having to deal with Sean questioning you every five minutes. That's the real bugbear, yes?"

"You can be too smart sometimes." Lorne laughed, ruffled Onyx's fur, and stood up to leave.

"I'll take that as a compliment," Carol said as they walked to the front door.

"Give me a ring over the weekend. Let me know how you're feeling, all right?"

"I will. Make sure you tell Charlie what I said about filling in for her next weekend. It'll do her good to get away. The poor child hasn't had a break in months."

"Crap. You're right. If anyone deserves a break, she does, especially after all the emotional crap she's had to endure with Henry's passing."

"Precisely, although Sheba has taken the sting out of that particular problem, hasn't she? Those two have a bright future ahead of them, once the real training begins."

"The obstacle course training? Do you really think that? I'd love her to have an outside interest. I'd prefer if it was away from the dogs. She's not been the same since she lost her friend last year. Tends to steer clear of going out with her mates now, fearing further problems, I guess."

"You're right. We've discussed it. Give her time. That's why I think she should take off for the weekend. She'll be right soon." Carol tapped her nose and winked at Lorne.

"What are you saying? That there's a new romance on the horizon?"

"Might be. Let her go to the training with Sheba, join the local dog training club, and we'll revisit this conversation after that, okay?"

"Interesting. I'd love her to settle down with a nice boy. She deserves to be happy more than any of us, after all she's encountered in her short life."

"She'll be fine. Don't force her. She'll find love when she's ready to accept it. Hey, look at it this way—if she does fall for a boy at the training club, at least you'll know he'll have a genuinely kind heart. Anyone who works with dogs has an abundance of love to give."

"That's so true. Right, I better get home and see what hubby has attempted to cook for dinner."

"You're in for a surprise," Carol called after her as she closed the door.

Lorne wasn't keen on that kind of surprise. Tony's prowess in the kitchen department was severely lacking at the best of times. *Maybe I should stop off at the chippie on the way home, just in case!*

When she walked through the back door of the house, billowing smoke greeted her. "Tony! Get in here, quick." Inserting her hand into the oven glove, she yanked open the oven door and wafted smoke away from her face.

"What? Shit! How could I forget that? Sorry, I was on the phone to Joe and…"

"Just get the bloody dish outside. No, leave me to do it. Open the back door for me."

Lorne removed the casserole dish from the oven and, with outstretched arms, carried it outside. She placed it on the gravel by the back door and turned the outside tap on to douse the flames.

"Another successful Tony dinner hits the dust," Charlie said.

Lorne shook her head. "I should be grateful he tries to help us out. Most men wouldn't."

Tony marched out of the house and called over his shoulder, "I'll be back in ten minutes."

Lorne and Charlie laughed. "Yeah, laden with fish and chips, I bet," Lorne retorted sarcastically.

After a chip-shop dinner, Charlie escaped to her room with Sheba, and Lorne and Tony snuggled up together on the couch. He started the conversation off with a complaint about how frustrating his day had been and how he hated questioning folks for a living.

"It goes with the territory, love. I don't know what you can do about it. How does Joe feel about that side of things? Maybe you could split the chores up? He questions people while you do all the research needed to crack the case. Would that work?"

Tony shook his head. "I don't think that would be fair. He feels the same way as I do about it."

"Poor you. You're so used to going into a situation with all guns ablazing. It's hard to change to a softly, softly approach, isn't it?"

He nodded.

Lorne kissed his cheek and added, "It will soon become second nature to you. Hang in there. You're doing a great job so far."

The music started for the nightly news programme, and they eagerly awaited the plea Karen had instructed the show to air. It turned out to be the final item just before the credits ran.

"Great, that was a half-hearted attempt to help on their part. What's the betting we get very little from that?"

"At least they aired it. Try not to be too dismissive about the plea yet, Lorne. What's on the agenda for this weekend?"

"Are you working at all?"

"No. Joe and I decided there wouldn't be any point. We'll hit the trail hard again on Monday morning."

"Same as us, really then. Well, I dropped in on Carol on the way home. She's not coming back to work at the kennels until Wednesday and has promised to give Charlie a break next weekend. I'm going to do my best to try and persuade Charlie to go away for a few days."

He glanced down at her through narrowed eyes. "And?"

"Well, I thought if we have a quiet time this weekend, we could make the most of having the house to ourselves next weekend when Charlie's away."

"You're presuming she will go away, of course."

"A couple of gentle persuasive remarks during the next few days will help sway her, I'm sure."

"Yeah, those kinds of remarks usually have a way of working their magic on me from time to time."

She kissed him hard on the mouth then snuggled up against his chest as the film, a romcom Charlie had picked out for them, started.

By the end of the weekend, Lorne had finally persuaded Charlie to go on a trip to Alton Towers with a friend of hers the following Saturday and Sunday, something she never thought she'd be able to do, given the objections that had tumbled out of her daughter's mouth. Now all she had to do was think up something special to do with her husband while Charlie was away. She had the rest of the week to figure out that particular problem.

CHAPTER ELEVEN

When the blue sky travelled with her on the way into work on Monday morning, Lorne had a good feeling about the day ahead of her. AJ, already at his desk, looked up when Lorne walked into the incident room. She could tell things weren't quite right by the way his shoulders slumped and the absence of his usual cheerful smile.

"Everything all right with Katy, AJ?"

"Still the same. Did you have a good weekend?"

"It was quiet. Come on. Let's have it?"

His smile appeared then, and he waved a sheet of paper under her nose. "This will brighten your day."

"You bloody wind-up merchant. What is it?" She read the handwritten note and let out a whoop of joy. "What have you done about it? Anything?"

"Nope, thought you'd prefer to deal with it when you arrived. Good news, yes?"

"The best we could hope for, I'd say. I'll be right back."

Lorne took the sheet of paper with her and trotted along the corridor to the chief's office.

His PA was sorting through a pile of post.

"Is he in? I have good news I'd like to share with him."

The PA looked down at her desk. "He's not on the phone at the moment. Go on. I'm sure he won't mind being interrupted."

"Thanks." Lorne knocked on Sean's door before she entered.

"Lorne? Come in. Do you have good news or bad?"

"You know me so well. Actually, this piece of news is of the pleasant variety." She placed the note on his desk in front of him.

Sean read it, looked up, and tilted his head. "Very interesting. What are you planning to do about it? Go and see this neighbour—this Mrs. Shaw—to corroborate what she's told us?"

"First up, we need to obtain a warrant for any addresses the Platts own. Just in case the neighbour is wrong about the work being carried out on their primary residence. Don't forget, I checked the place thoroughly myself. So far, the team haven't uncovered info relating to them owning anything other than the property they live in."

"Okay, then that could prove difficult. What if they've purchased another property in her maiden name? Have you looked into that? Or have they inherited a house from any relatives? Perhaps they haven't transferred the names over on the deeds yet," Sean suggested, to Lorne's surprise.

"Good thinking. I have another idea, one that we should chase up this morning while the team are busy searching for that information."

"Oh? Well, don't stop there."

Lorne crossed her arms and leaned her hip against the edge of his desk. "When I spoke to the woman at social services the other day, she mentioned the Platts had a grown-up son. I reckon we should pay him a visit. Then I think we should go and see the neighbour, Mrs. Shaw, just to clarify what she's rung in and informed us about. For all we know, it could turn out that she has some kind of vendetta against the family."

"You're right. Do we know the son's name?" Sean asked.

"No. Very remiss of me. I forgot to ask the other day. I'll ring the woman back ASAP."

"Okay, with regard to the neighbour, why don't you send one of the guys out to take down a statement? It will help us time-wise. Not only that, if the Platts see us turn up there to talk to a neighbour, it might raise their suspicions and cause them to abscond."

"I'll send Stephen and Graham. AJ and Karen prefer to do the office side of things anyway. When do you want to head off?"

"Give me fifteen minutes. How's that?"

"Suits me." Lorne returned to the incident room. The rest of the team had arrived, and she filled them in on what had transpired.

"Stephen and Graham, I need you to use your discretion and go and see the Platts' neighbour, Mrs. Shaw, to get a statement. Be careful. I'd advise taking a clipboard or something with you just to put the Platts off the scent if they happen to observe you arriving."

"Sure," Stephen replied. "So, this lady said she's seen the tradesmen enter the house or not?"

"Yes, she didn't mention whether they conducted any work there or whether she saw their vans turn up and the men just meet up with the Platts at the property. She was a little vague in that respect, so that's what we need to ascertain. Plus, please bear in mind that I searched the address myself and didn't see any signs of any work going on there."

"Right, leave it with us. Do you want us to go now?"

"Yep, the sooner you get over there the better. I'll be leaving with the chief in five minutes or so. We'll compare notes when we get back and go from there."

Lorne searched her desk for a name and extension number then picked up the phone. "Hello, Ms. Murray. This is Lorne Warner from the Met. We spoke the other day regarding the Platts."

"I remember. What can I do for you?"

"During our conversation, you mentioned in passing that the Platts have an older child. I don't suppose you can tell me his name and perhaps supply me with his address?"

"Sure, hold on while I get the information for you."

Lorne heard the phone hit the desk, a metal drawer to what she presumed was a filing cabinet open, and the sound of paper being shuffled before the woman picked up the phone again. "Here it is. Denis Platt. He lives at 42 Cresswell Road in Islington."

"Not far from his parents' house then. Thanks, that's a great help."

Lorne hung up and called over to AJ to ask him to conduct a detailed background check on the son. The phone on her desk rang. "Hello, DS... umm, I mean Acting Detective Inspector Warner speaking."

"Hi, Lorne. It's Patti. Just wanted to update you on the PMs I've performed to do with your case."

"Hi, Patti. That's great. I was going to give you a ring later anyway."

"Oh, about what?"

"The case. We've got a couple of suspects in mind."

"Excellent news. So you'll be requiring my team to carry out a DNA search of the suspects' property, is that right?"

"Exactly. We're in the process of getting a warrant now. That could take a few days to be approved, so we're chomping at the bit at this end. What did the PMs reveal? Anything unexpected?"

"Not really. The first two confirmed that both victims died before the fumes could take effect. Looking at the wounds on all three victims, it looks like the same weapon was used. Maybe the weapon will show up at the suspects' house."

"Let's hope so. I met the couple yesterday, went to see them with the chief, and they seemed really shifty to me." She lowered her voice and added, "Not that the chief picked up anything out of place."

Patti laughed. "Typical of a paper-pusher! I bet he's driving you around the bend by now."

"So-so. He's not being too dim so far. I better go. We're off to visit the suspects' son. I'll call you the second we get the warrant. Perhaps we can all show up at the house at the same time."

"Sounds like a plan. Good luck with the visit."

As Lorne hung up, Sean Roberts entered the room. He clapped his hands. "Come on, Acting Inspector, get a wriggle on. Places to go, people to see, *et cetera.*"

Lorne shook her head at his jovial manner. She sensed a day of annoyance ahead of her. "I'm primed and ready to go." She turned her attention to the team. "If you find out anything interesting, give me a call, okay?"

AJ and Karen nodded their agreement. Lorne followed the chief out of the incident room and the station. Once in the car, she punched in the address to the sat nav and sat back as Sean drove. He tried to make small talk during the journey—mostly talking about what his wife, Carmen, and their baby daughter got up to over the weekend—but Lorne was only half-listening. Her mind was totally focused on the questions she wanted to ask Denis Platt when they got to his house, if he was at home. She cursed herself for not bothering to find out where he worked, and she knew that Sean would tease her about her absentmindedness once the truth came out.

The address turned out to be a terraced house that looked as though it had been divided into a couple of flats, as there were two doorbells at the side of the doorframe. The top flat appeared to be the one they were after. Lorne rang the bell. Sean nudged her in the ribs and pointed up to a woman looking out of the window in the flat above. The woman disappeared, and Lorne heard someone coming down the stairs. A young brunette opened the door. She wore subtle makeup and was dressed in jeans and a snug-fitting pink T-shirt.

"Yes?"

Lorne flashed her ID. "Sorry to trouble you. I'm Acting Inspector Lorne Warner, and this is my boss, DCI Sean Roberts. Is Denis Platt in, please?"

The woman's brow wrinkled with concern. "He is. Can I ask what this is about? He's just getting ready for work."

"We won't keep him long, I promise. It's concerning a case we're working on." Lorne smiled at the woman.

"Just a moment. I'll see if he has time to see you." She closed the door, leaving them standing on the doorstep, bathing in the warm morning sun.

"I think we should be cautious, not show our hands too soon with the son."

"I'll leave the questioning to you then. The last thing we want is for the son to ring the parents and warn them."

"My sentiments exactly. It's going to be tricky, and there are no guarantees that won't happen." Lorne heard someone coming down the stairs and raised a finger to her lips.

The woman opened the door and invited them in. "He can spare you ten minutes before he leaves."

"Where does Denis work?" Lorne asked, following the woman up the stairs, with Sean bringing up the rear.

"He works in a care home. Loves his job. Loves caring for people who can't care for themselves."

"He's to be admired. Many people I know would struggle working in a role like that."

"I say the same thing. You should hear some of the tales he tells when he comes home. He's such a sensitive soul. He'd love to bring a handful of his patients back here every night and continue caring for them if he had the choice." She paused midway up the flight of stairs and turned to face them. "He finds it hard to trust the carers on the nightshift. I keep telling him he can't be on duty twenty-four hours a day." She continued walking.

"He sounds a very considerate kind of man."

They entered the lounge, where toys were strewn across the floor, and a man in his early-thirties was hurriedly trying to tidy them away. "Sorry about the mess."

Lorne smiled. "How many have you got?"

"Kids? None. My siblings frequently visit and tend to take over the place, or should I say try and destroy the flat when they're here," Denis replied, smiling.

Lorne mentally stored that piece of information away and only nodded a response.

"Please take a seat. Sam said you wanted a word with me."

Lorne and Sean sat on the couch, and Denis sat in an easy chair. Sam remained at the doorway to the lounge, resting against the doorframe with her arms folded.

Cautiously, Lorne began. "We're investigating a sensitive crime that has taken place near your parents' home. Can I ask how close you are to your parents?"

Denis immediately glanced over at his girlfriend. She smiled and nodded reassuringly at him.

"We've had our differences over the years. Why do you ask?"

"To be honest, I'm going to lay my cards on the table with you from the word go."

"Okay."

Lorne shuffled to the edge of her seat, purposely touching her leg to Sean's as she continued, "We visited your parents' house yesterday, in connection with this crime, and well, let's just say we left there feeling very dissatisfied."

"In what way? Hang on, what sort of crime are we talking about?" Denis asked.

Sam walked across the room and sat on the arm of her boyfriend's chair, and they linked hands.

Lorne inhaled and exhaled a large breath. "Actually, there have been three crimes committed. We believe the victims were murdered."

"What? And you think my parents have something to do with these murders?"

Lorne noticed the way the couple's hands tightened. She felt Sean's leg press against her own. She wasn't sure if it was a warning not to continue. Maybe she had said too much already. She didn't think so—she had a feeling she could trust this man, though she wasn't sure why. "We're not sure, to be honest. We have evidence of a vehicle similar to the one your parents own being used in the crimes. One question, if I may?"

Denis nodded.

"Do your parents own another home?"

"No. Why?"

"Okay, then have your parents conducted any form of renovations on their family home in the last few weeks?"

"Not that I know of. I'm confused. What does that have to do with the crimes you mentioned?"

Lorne's mobile rang. She pulled it from her jacket pocket and saw the caller was Stephen. "Sorry, this is important." Lorne gave Sean an apologetic smile and rushed into the hallway. "This better be important," she said into the phone.

"It is, boss—very."

"Let's have it then, Stephen."

"We've just finished taking a statement from Mrs. Shaw, and she raised an interesting point that we seemed to have overlooked, boss."

Lorne exhaled an impatient breath. "Which is, Stephen?"

"When I asked if she had actually seen the tradesmen enter the house with their tools, she looked at me as if I was crazy. 'Of course,' she said, adamantly. When I told her that you had searched the house and found no such work had taken place, she scratched her head and said she couldn't understand that at all."

"Get to the point, Stephen. We're questioning the son, and he has to leave for work soon."

"Sorry. Okay, I then asked Mrs. Shaw if she'd heard any noise coming from inside the house when this supposed work was taking place, and she admitted she'd heard a lot of noise, especially when she was in the back garden."

"Meaning what? They have another building in the garden that I missed?"

"No. She seems to think it was taking place in the cellar."

"Shit! A cellar? I didn't have a clue those houses had a cellar. Shit!"

"Neither did we! The thing is, you wouldn't know looking at the front elevation of the house. Go around the back, and it's a different matter. Graham and I snuck around the back alley and spotted that five out of the seven properties in that row have another level."

"Good work, Stephen. Are you heading back to the station now?"

"Yep, unless you want us to do anything else?"

"Nope. We shouldn't be long here. See you later."

Lorne disconnected the call and opened the lounge door. Sean glanced her way. "Can I see you for a second, sir?"

Sean joined her in the hallway and leaned in close to whisper, "So much for not giving too much away. What the fuck was that all about in there, Lorne?"

"Forget about that for a second. That was Stephen with some very interesting news about the parents' house."

"Okay, you've got my attention. This better be good, Lorne."

Lorne pulled a face at him. "It is. They have a cellar."

Sean's eyes protruded. "What? Were you aware of that?"

Lorne growled. "Of course I wasn't bloody aware of it. But it makes sense, doesn't it?"

"Shit. I hope your cock-up doesn't land us in a pile of shit, Sergeant. You should never have divulged what you have to Denis and his girlfriend. Never." He chastised her, neglecting to refer to her proper title, the one he'd forced her to take.

"Don't you see, Sean? He's different from them. Look at the career path he's chosen to take."

"What? Are you insane, woman? What the effing hell does that have to do with anything?" He pointed at her. "Are you forgetting that the parents are foster parents? The same could be said about them for goodness's sake."

Lorne shook her head. "All right then. Let's see what your powers of observation are like. Spot the difference between the two homes?"

"Doh! One's a three-storey house, as we've just discovered, and this is a bloody flat."

"That's good, for starters. Now really give the question some consideration." Lorne tapped her foot and crossed her arms impatiently as her anger heated her cheeks.

Sean's mouth turned down at the sides, and he shook his head in resignation. "Nope, nothing is springing to mind. What are you getting at?"

"The tidiness of the two properties. Anyone would think that Denis and Sam were the foster parents, *not* the other way round. Don't tell me you didn't spot that the minute we arrived?"

"Can't say I did. How strange. I wonder how often the kids stay here? You said even their bedrooms at the Platts' home were immaculate, right?"

"Yep. There's more to this than is currently apparent. The question is how do we proceed now?"

"Ask them outright? How often the kids stay here? Why they stay here? Denis also said that his parents hadn't done any renovations to their property lately, either. What's that all about? If the neighbour knows, how is it that Denis doesn't?"

"Which is why I think we can trust him."

Sean sucked in a breath and pulled a face.

"Don't look like that, Sean. You said yourself, it seems strange how he doesn't know work has gone on at the house."

"What if he's lying? Being purposefully evasive? I wouldn't show all your cards just yet, Lorne. Not until we have that warrant in hand *and* had a chance to investigate the house exhaustively."

"So, what are you suggesting? That we terminate this meeting now?"

"Why not? He's in a rush to get to work anyway. My advice would be just to change direction and only ask about the kids, then leave."

Lorne chewed her bottom lip. "I don't like it, but I do understand where you're coming from. Maybe I am guilty of letting him know too much—I hope not. He has a kind face, unlike his parents."

Sean snorted. "Oh, that makes perfect sense then."

"Piss off, Sean… I mean, sir."

Sean turned her around and nudged her in the back, pushing her gently into the lounge. "Sorry, something urgent has come up concerning another case. We have to leave unfortunately," Lorne said, smiling at the young couple.

"I have to finish getting ready for work anyway," Denis replied. He smiled and stood up.

"One last question, if I may?" Lorne asked.

"Sure."

"How often do your siblings stay here with you?"

"It varies. Anything from a couple of times a week to once a month. I'm happy to have them here, Inspector."

"Thank you. I'm glad they have you to look out for them. Would you mind keeping this conversation private, for the time being at least? Just until our investigations have run their course."

"Okay, providing you'll keep us informed of your findings. If my parents are guilty of something, I'd like to know about it from you. I've been fair with you. Can I ask you be as fair with me in return?"

Lorne held out her hand and shook Denis's firmly as an unspoken message crossed the divide between them. "You have my word. Thank you for your time. We'll be in touch soon."

Sam showed Lorne and Sean back down the stairs. Before they got back in the car, Lorne looked up at the window of the flat and saw a pensive Denis staring at her. Lorne waved and jumped in the passenger seat.

"He holds a very dark secret close to his heart, that one," Lorne stated quietly.

"You think?"

"I know. Look at his reaction when I said about his parents' car being involved in a suspected crime. It was far from natural."

CHAPTER TWELVE

To keep her mind off the fact that the Magistrate was taking an eternity to issue the warrant, Lorne threw herself into the paperwork strewn across Katy's desk. She had given the team clear instructions that the second they received the call from the court, they should interrupt her immediately.

Just after lunch, Lorne's mobile rang. It was Tony. "Hi, sweetheart. This is a surprise."

"Not a pleasant one, either, when you hear what I have to say."

Lorne sat back in her chair and stared out the window at the cloudless blue sky overhead. "I'm listening."

"I might be a little late tonight."

"That's okay. You don't usually ring me with that kind of news. Why this time?"

"Joe and I have decided to hire some frog suits and search the river."

Lorne bounced upright in her chair. "Are you *crazy*?"

Tony laughed. "I don't think so. We're not going into this blind, love. We're trained in this type of exercise. Admittedly, it was a few years ago, but nevertheless, we're assuming it will be like riding a bike. Anyway, we've hired all the equipment now. Trust me—I know what I'm doing."

Lorne bit down hard on the retort threatening to tumble out of her mouth. *Yes, you might have dived before, but that was when you were able-bodied. You're forgetting about your prosthetic leg!*

"Don't go all quiet on me, Lorne. I know what you're thinking. I'll be fine. Joe will be with me every step of the way. If I didn't feel up to tackling the mission, I wouldn't do it. Trust me, all right?" he asked for a second time.

Lorne covered the phone with her hand and exhaled a large breath, then she said, "All right. I'll *trust* you. Only if you promise to ring me after you finish the manoeuvre."

"I promise. Ring you later." He blew her a kiss that melted her heart.

"Take care. Love you." She hung up and again glanced out the window, thankful that it was a calm, warm day for Tony's exploits.

Sean Roberts walked into the office. "You look pensive. Anything you want to share?" He sat down in the chair opposite.

"Tony called to say he's undertaking a dangerous exercise today. I could throttle that man sometimes," she replied light-heartedly.

"He's a tough guy, Lorne. I'm sure he wouldn't put himself in any unnecessary danger. He knows you'd kill him."

"Ha, bloody, ha. Did you need something?"

"Not really. Just sitting around, twiddling my thumbs in my office. Thought I'd come over here and bug the hell out of you instead."

"You're all heart. I tell you what you can do." She grinned broadly.

"Uh-oh, not sure I'm going to like this. What mundane task do you want me to do?"

"You could use your influence and chase up the warrant for me. If I place the call, it usually ends up at the bottom of the pile."

He glared at her through narrowed eyes. "Is that all I'm useful for?"

She winked at him. "No. I hear you're also good at treating Acting DIs to a well-earned cup of coffee now and then, too. Milk with one sugar. Thanks."

He pushed out of the chair and mumbled something incoherent under his breath. He left the office and returned with a vending-machine coffee for her. "I'll see what I can do with regard to the other order you issued."

"It was merely a request," she reminded him, fluttering her eyelashes.

Sean reappeared around ten minutes later just as Lorne was signing off on yet another head office change of procedure. She put the form in the in-tray for Katy's attention upon her return. "Well?" she asked, more out of hope than expectation.

"Grab your jacket. We have instructions to pick the warrant up in fifteen minutes."

"Wow! Really? How did you manage that? No, wait, I'd rather not know if it involves you dishing out sexual favours."

Sean tried to look annoyed at her remark but ended up cracking into a toothy smile instead. "Cheeky mare. It's done. There's no need for you to know the ins and outs."

"That's great. I really appreciate your astonishing powers of persuasion, Sean. Let's rally the troops then. I want to go in there heavy-handed. We'll take Stephen and Graham with us. Can you let them know? I'll ring Patti and get her to meet us at the address with her team."

Sean left the office, and Lorne reached for the phone. "Patti, it's me. We've got the go-ahead. Can you join us at this address?" She reeled off the Platts' address.

"As it happens, I'm between PMs right now. Are you heading over there now?"

"We are. I'll see you there. Thanks, Patti."

When Lorne and Sean arrived at the property, Patti's van pulled up at virtually the same time. Stephen and Graham joined them a few seconds later.

Lorne turned her back on the house. "Okay, I've already spotted Mrs. Platt at the window. She'll realise something is up with us arriving in a convoy. Be ready for it to kick off. Let's go."

Lorne approached the house with the rest of the team a few steps behind her. Then she thumped her fist on the front door. When the door remained unanswered, Lorne opened the letterbox and called out, "We know you're in there, Mrs. Platt. I saw you." She stood up again. After she received no reply, Lorne instructed Stephen and Graham to go round the rear of the property.

Lorne watched her two colleagues jog up a nearby alley, then she strained her ear against the front door. Eventually, she heard both male and female voices shouting, and what sounded like the back door being broken down. "I think they're in. Shall we break the front door down, too?" she asked Sean.

Without replying, he gently pushed Lorne aside and shoulder-barged the door, only to rebound off it and cry out in pain. "Ouch!"

"Get out of the way, Sean," she told him, trying to keep the amusement out of her tone. The bottom half of the door was made up of two separate panels. Lorne recognised those as the weakest points of the door. She turned to face Patti and her team, spread her arms out either side to hold onto the brick façade surrounding the entrance, and kicked her heel at the door. It took several attempts to splinter the wood. Sean took over then; he knelt and squeezed his hand through the door, hoping to find the lock low enough on the inside. He failed, but Stephen opened the door not long after to let them in. They rushed through the house to find Mrs. Platt sitting at the kitchen table, her head buried in her hands.

"The husband? Is he around?" Lorne asked Graham, standing behind the woman.

Graham shook his head. "Haven't seen him, boss."

"Mrs. Platt, where's your husband?"

She raised her head and glared at Lorne through narrowed, cold eyes for a few seconds before she spat on the floor, missing Lorne's feet by inches. *Hmm... and there was me thinking you were a house-proud bitch!*

"I'll ask you one final time. *Where* is your husband?"

"Out," the woman bit back venomously.

Lorne observed her long and hard—she was lying. Lorne turned and whispered in Sean's ear. "She's lying. We need to find the entrance to the cellar and quickly, before he destroys any evidence."

"Okay, leave her to me. Where do you think the entrance is?"

Lorne sucked the inside of her mouth. "No idea." She turned to look at the suspect and watched her eyes intently for a while. Every now and then, they wandered off to the right, towards the back door. Lorne walked over to the sink and threw back the carpet runner to reveal a trap door. "Here! Sean, Stephen, come with me. Graham, watch her like a hawk. Tie her to the chair if she gives you any problems."

Lorne eased open the door and peered down the hole.

"Run, Courtney, run," Mrs. Platt warned her husband.

Lorne felt like swiping the smug look off the woman's face. "You'll regret doing that, Mrs. Platt," she said, then descended the stairs, pepper spray in hand, after the other suspect. Sean and Stephen clomped down the stairs in hot pursuit after her. When they reached the bottom, it was evident all the renovation work had taken place down there. Mr. Platt was nowhere to be seen, though. Lorne touched her lips with her finger, telling the two men to be quiet, while they listened for any form of noise giving away the man's hiding place.

A slight noise at the rear of the room caught her attention. She tiptoed towards the area, her finger on the top of the spray. Sean and Stephen moved with her. Lorne pointed at a small door as they rounded the corner. Her two colleagues nodded. Lorne reached for the ancient brass doorknob and slowly turned it. She was surprised it moved. Suddenly, the door flew open, and Mr. Platt ran at them, a metal bar raised above his head. He was screaming, his eyes blazing like an inferno, his mouth twisted into an angry snarl.

"Fuck off, the lot of you," he shouted, swinging the bar in front of him.

Stephen and Sean separated and jumped on the man. Stephen wrestled with his arm, trying to disarm him. Once they'd grappled Platt to the ground, Lorne jumped up and down on his forearm until he relinquished his grip on his weapon. She removed the cuffs from her pocket and slapped one on his flailing wrist. Sean and Stephen gripped his other arm and pulled it down to meet his other one. Lorne encircled his wrist in the other cuff, and they all let out a sigh of relief. The man cursed continually until they forced him up the stairs. Mrs. Platt left her chair and ran to her husband, throwing her arms around his neck and kissing his cheek over and over again. Lorne felt sickened by the display of affection. The only saving grace she could see was that Mr. Platt instantly calmed down when he was in his wife's arms. She would never understand the meaning of such a volatile love.

Patti stepped forward and squeezed Lorne's arm. "You done good, girl. Is it all right if we start our examination now?"

Eyeing the couple, watching their response, Lorne nodded. "Why not? The sooner we get on with things, the quicker we can throw these two behind bars."

"For what? Having a cellar?" Mr. Platt let out the worst demented laugh Lorne had ever heard a suspect let loose.

"We'll see, shall we? Get her away from him," Lorne said, ordering Graham and Stephen to separate the suspects. Just then, another person entered the kitchen from the hallway. Lorne was surprised to see who the visitor was. "Denis? What are you doing here?"

"Do you know her? How do you know her?" his mother demanded.

Denis's gaze remained on Lorne; the young man seemed confused. "She called me. Said I had to come over here and help them. I had no idea what she was talking about. Are you arresting them?"

"Yes, Denis. Do you want to talk in the front room?"

He nodded, and Lorne motioned for him to go ahead of her. She closed the door behind them and pointed at the sofa. When they were seated, Lorne noted how much Denis's hands were shaking. He tried hard to disguise the trembling, but Lorne spotted it easily. "Are you all right, Denis?"

"I'm confused. I have been for years."

"Confused about what, Denis?"

He inhaled a shuddering breath and turned to face her. Tears glistened in his eyes, threatening to spill onto his cheek. Lorne placed her hand on top of his. "I know you're not part of this Denis, if that is what's worrying you. I can recognise an innocent man when I see one."

"Thank you. Be careful of them. They're manipulative. My whole life has been one of manipulation. The minute I think I've found peace, this happens. Lorne, I have one favour to ask of you."

"What's that, Denis?"

"Please, please let Sam and I look after the children. Please don't let them go back into care. They trust us. They haven't opened up to us yet, but I think it will only be a matter of time. They need us, need a loving home, someone they can trust not to..."

"Not to what, Denis?"

"I've said too much. Please give me your assurance that you'll do everything you can to let me take the kids home?"

"I have no jurisdiction over what social services do, Denis. By all means, I can have a word on your behalf. But seriously, do you think you're up to looking after the children?"

"Yes, I'm up to the job. They spend most of their time with us anyway."

Lorne rose from the sofa, aware she needed to get the Platts back to the station and interviewed. That had to be her number one priority. "Look, let me sort things out with your parents first, then I'll give the lady at social services a ring. All I can say is I'll do my very best for you." She handed him one of her business cards. "I'll give you a call later. Denis, ring me if you need to talk to anyone, okay?"

"Thank you. What charges are you arresting them on?" he asked quietly, his eyes cast down to the floor.

"Murder."

His head snapped up, and his gaze met Lorne's. "Murder? Both of them?"

"Unless one of them tells us the other person wasn't involved, yes."

"Murder," Denis mumbled quietly again and shook his head.

"I have to get on now, Denis."

He shook hands with Lorne then walked with her out of the lounge, but instead of following her into the kitchen to where his parents were, Denis left the house by the front door.

CHAPTER THIRTEEN

Lorne joined the rest of the team in the kitchen. The Platts' hands were behind their backs, locked in cuffs, and Stephen and Graham were guarding them.

"Down here, Lorne," Patti called out.

Lorne and Sean rushed back down the stairs to the cellar. Patti was standing at the entrance to the cupboard where Mr. Platt had sprung from, shining a torch inside. Two members of Patti's team stood aside for Lorne and Sean to take their places.

"My God!" Lorne covered her mouth for a second then asked, "How long has that been there?"

Patti shook her head in despair. "Until I examine the skeleton thoroughly, I won't have an accurate answer for you, Lorne. I can give a rough guestimate if you like? Years."

Sean cleared his throat. "Could the tradesmen have seen this? Is that why they were killed? Because they discovered it?"

"You could be on to something there, Sean. If the Platts assumed the men had seen the skeleton, then they probably panicked and thought the men would notify the police once they left the house."

"So they killed three men because of *this*?" Patti asked. "It seems a little unbelievable. If the first man had looked in the cupboard, why invite more men down here, knowing that they might witness the same?"

"Perhaps they got a thrill out of killing Paul Lee and then purposefully enticed the others down here, confident they could catch them off guard and kill them, too," Lorne suggested quietly in case her voice travelled up the stairs and the Platts might overhear.

"This can now be regarded as a serial killer case, I take it?" Sean said.

"Three murders that we know of and an actual skeleton in a cupboard. I think that's a pretty darn accurate assumption, boss," Lorne agreed.

"And that's just the start. Look around you. Do we know what lies beneath these renovations?"

Lorne gasped. "God, don't say that, Patti. Isn't four bodies enough?"

"It's something we can't discount at this point, Lorne. We'll get the gear in over the next few days and see what we can find."

"Next few days? You anticipate your guys being here that long?" Sean asked, surprised.

"You want us to be thorough, don't you, DCI Roberts?" Patti replied sharply.

Lorne stifled a giggle at the pathologist's put-down as the colour rose in Sean's cheeks. "Sorry, of course. What's next?" he asked.

"Well, I suggest you get on with your side of the job and leave me and my team to tear this place apart. I think I'm going to need reinforcements to handle this, though."

Lorne tugged Sean's sleeve. "Thanks, Patti. Good luck. Let me know what you find. I'll be tied up for the next day or two, questioning the suspects. You've got my mobile number?"

"I have. I bet you're finished before we are."

Lorne and Sean climbed the stairs again and received the evil eye from both the Platts when they entered the kitchen. Lorne shook her head in disgust. "Get them in the cars, boys. We'll take Mr. Platt with us, okay?"

Back at the station, the desk sergeant read the two suspects their rights and informed them that a solicitor would be provided, if they didn't have the money to fund one for themselves. The suspects remained silent, so the duty sergeant put in a request for a solicitor to attend. While they waited for the solicitor to arrive, the suspects were put in separate cells. The instant Lorne stepped into the incident room, she picked up the phone and dialled social services to talk to Ms. Murray, the woman dealing with the Platts.

"Hello, Ms. Murray. This is Acting DI Warner at the Met. We spoke the other day."

"I remember. What can I do for you, Inspector?"

"I'm ringing up to tell you there has been a development since we last spoke. We've just arrested the Platts for murder."

The woman gasped. "What? You're kidding me?"

"No, I'm *deadly* serious. I was ringing up to let you know that Denis and his girlfriend would like to take care of the children."

"That's not possible. The children will be placed in emergency care."

"I know there are procedures you have to follow, but I do think you should allow Denis to care for the children. They know him, after all."

"Are you serious? You've just told me his parents are murderers, and you want the kids to remain within the same family? I find that incredible, Inspector."

"His parents might be killers, but Denis is as genuine as they come, Ms. Murray. Have you ever met the young man?"

"No, I haven't. I will have to put your proposal forward to my superiors. I wouldn't hold my breath on receiving a positive outcome if I were you."

"What will happen to the children then? You told me the only reason the kids were placed with the Platts in the first place was because you're short of suitable foster homes at present, wasn't it?"

"Things change rapidly. I have no idea at this stage without looking at our files. We'll arrange for the children to be picked up from school. I'll have to go now and organise that ASAP as the school will be finishing for the day soon. Thank you for the information, Inspector. Leave the children's welfare to me."

"Umm… before you hang up. I'll be expecting you to come into the station to give a statement in the next day or two."

"Statement? About what?"

The woman's tone annoyed Lorne considerably. "About the number of visits you've made to the Platts' home over the last few months. I'd like it documented that you didn't find anything wrong with the fact the house was immaculate in spite of three young kids living there."

The woman tutted. "Really? Because there are no toys strewn about the place, you think that should highlight the children not being cared for properly? Have you heard yourself?"

"Let's put it this way—I thought at least half of your job was to be observant. If the situation jumped out to me as being suspicious, Ms. Murray, then I find it absolutely incredulous it didn't place a seed of doubt in your mind."

"You really have no idea about the sights I see, Inspector. Please do *not* judge me."

"I'm not judging you personally, Ms. Murray. However, I do believe the system is at fault when something like this is completely ignored."

"You're unbelievable. Spend a day with me, Inspector, and then see if you are willing to make the same accusation. I need to get on now. Like I said the other day, we're understaffed here."

"Very well. I will be ringing your superior myself to put across my request for Denis to look after the children, though, all the same."

"Do as you please," the woman said before she abruptly hung up.

"Aggghhh! Some people are so damn infuriating. Bloody woman has no idea."

Sean approached the desk, grinning. "Calm down. What was that about?"

"The woman at social services is refusing to let the kids stay with Denis."

"I'm inclined to agree with her."

"What?" Lorne pushed back her chair. It clattered against the desk behind. "I'm telling you this from the word go, Sean, that man had nothing to do with these killings. If anything, he *despises* his parents. Why, I have no idea, but he does."

"Has he told you that?"

"Not in so many words. I know simply by reading his body language when he's in the same room as them. Once I've gained his trust, I'm sure he'll be a key witness in his parents' downfall."

"So *that's* why you're bending over backwards to help him get the kids."

"I'm not *using* him, if that's what you're insinuating. Let's not fall out about this, Sean. He's different to them. Any idiot can see that."

"Well, this idiot can't see it, Lorne. I think it would cause irreparable harm to those kids if social services placed them with Denis. I also think you should back off and not cause any ill-feeling with that department, too."

Seething, Lorne swept her hair over her shoulder and headed for Katy's office. "Thanks for the advice," she called back before slamming the door after her. Once seated, she picked up the phone and immediately dialled Ms. Murray's head of department, despite Sean's warning.

Mr. Wenlock apparently had been pre-warned by Ms. Murray that Lorne would be making contact with him.

"Ah, Acting Detective Inspector Warner. Yes, I'm well aware of the case you're referring to, and no, I don't agree with you lambasting a member of my staff."

"Lambasting? I hardly did that, Mr. Wenlock. All I asked was for Ms. Murray to consider placing the children with someone they are comfortable with. In my eyes, that person would be Denis Platt."

"Unfortunately, that decision is not down to you. It will be taken by this department. I'm requesting that you leave us to do our job. Over the years we've been quite successful at it."

A recent number of cases highlighted in the media where SS had gravely let down children in their care—notably in Oxford, Rochdale, and Bradford—sprang to Lorne's mind. Fearing she wasn't getting anywhere fast, she decided it would be wiser not to press the issue. "Okay, I hear you, Mr. Wenlock, but please grant me this, that the three children will be homed together."

"That I can't guarantee, Inspector."

"It would be guaranteed if Denis took them in," she said, persistently making her point.

"We need to put it forward at the next group meeting. At this moment, I'm not ruling anything out. The more you push, the more likely the decision will go against you, Inspector. Was there anything else I can help you with today?"

"No. You've been most considerate. I'm sorry if I'm coming across as obstinate. I tend to do that where children and their safety are concerned."

"I understand. I assure you I will think carefully about your request. Goodbye, Inspector."

Lorne exhaled and puffed out her cheeks. She hung up only for the phone to ring straight away. "Hello, DS Warner," she replied out of habit.

"Ma'am, it's the desk sergeant. I'm ringing up to inform you that the solicitor has arrived."

"Only one?"

"Yes, ma'am."

"Okay, I'll be right down." Lorne left the office and spotted Sean standing in front of the incident board. She walked up to him and tapped him on the shoulder. "The brief is here. Do you want to sit in on the interviews?"

"Of course. You said brief, as in singular?"

"That's right. I thought we'd start with Mr. Platt first, agreed?"

"I concur. Do you intend playing one off against the other?" Sean asked, turning to face her.

"I would do if two solicitors had shown up. That's far more difficult to do when there's only one. He's going to know what the other suspect has said and no doubt take pleasure in shooting us down in flames."

"Why don't you demand another one?"

"I think I will when we get down there on the grounds of the solicitor wasting time."

"Yep, good call. Although, we have arrested them already due to our findings. Once they've been questioned, we can ship them out on remand, can't we?" Sean asked.

"The longer we can keep them here, the better. That way, we can question them more. Maybe they'll surprise us both by admitting their roles in the crimes without us having to use too much pressure," Lorne said.

"He looks the obstinate type. Regarding her, I'm not so sure. One minute she looks as though she's about to burst into tears, and the next, she gives you the impression she wouldn't think twice about ripping your throat out."

"Yeah, I noticed. Maybe she's mentally unstable. What's the betting they both try and pull that card somewhere down the line."

"If they do, it'll be another nail in social services' coffin, won't it? They check folks' medical backgrounds before even contemplating placing kids with them, right?"

"I presume it works like that." Lorne gasped and shook her head.

"What is it?"

"I've just had the most dreadful thought. What if the three kids heard the couple killing the men?"

"Presuming the men were killed at the property in the first instant," Sean acknowledged thoughtfully. "It doesn't bear thinking about."

"We'll try not to go down that route then. Let's remain focused on what the Platts did to their victims and go from there."

CHAPTER FOURTEEN

As it was almost five o'clock, Lorne quickly rang home and spoke to Charlie before she set off to interview the suspects. She warned her daughter that she wouldn't be home for hours and to go ahead and eat without her.

Lorne took a deep breath, preparing herself for the first interview. Then together, she and Sean made their way down the stairs.

"He's first, right?" Sean verified.

"Yep. I bet the first words out of his mouth are 'no comment.'"

Sean chuckled. "And the last, no doubt. We need an element of surprise to get a reaction from him."

"Yeah, I know. I've been wracking my brains, but I haven't come up with anything logical so far. It's going to be a case of suppressing our frustration and smiling a lot. That usually pisses them off enough to get a reaction. Just follow my lead. That is, if I'm to lead the questioning?"

"Of course. I wouldn't have a clue where to start."

They made their way down the corridor to Interview Room One. Courtney Platt was already seated at the table, his cuffed hands clenched together until the whites of his knuckles showed. He slowly turned to face them. Platt's eyes narrowed and homed in on Lorne's. She smiled to combat the creepy sensation rippling along her spine.

After introducing herself and the chief to the young male solicitor, Mr. Jenson, Lorne set the tape running and gave the usual spiel—date, time, names of those present in the room, and what crime the suspect was being questioned about.

"So, Mr. Platt, can you tell us why you were hiding in your cellar when we called at your property today?"

Platt said through gritted teeth, "No comment."

Lorne's smile broadened, and she turned her attention to Jenson. "Just for the record, we found your client in a store cupboard in the cellar. He attacked us when he was discovered. Would an innocent person do that, in your opinion, Mr. Jenson?"

Jenson raised an eyebrow. "Your questions should be aimed at my client, Inspector, not me."

"Indeed, Mr. Jenson. Just for the record, after your client came out of the cupboard, our team of forensics found a skeleton sitting inside. Nice company your client keeps, eh?"

Again Jenson's eyebrow rose, then he shrugged and looked down at his notebook.

Ignorant shit! "We'll see if your wife can enlighten us on that count after we've finished questioning you, Mr. Platt." Lorne beamed as if the suspect was a very old, dear friend of hers.

Platt responded by inhaling deeply and tutting in disgust.

"Okay, we'll come back to the skeleton part of the case later and now get to the real reason you were arrested today, Mr. Platt. When did the renovations begin on your home?"

"No comment."

"I used to renovate houses for a living myself at one stage and know the sequence in which the tradesmen carry out their tasks. Bearing that in mind, I would hazard a guess at Paul Lee laying the electrics at your property around two weeks ago. Is that when he began?"

"No comment."

"Did you find his work faulty? Is that why you killed him?" Lorne asked, her gaze never faltering from Platt's and her smile set firmly in place.

"No comment," Platt spat out with a snarl.

"Did you kill him because you couldn't afford to pay his bill? That seems a little extreme to me."

"No comment."

"Or was it because Mr. Lee discovered the skeleton you had stored in the cupboard?"

Platt's eyes flickered shut for a moment then reopened; his gaze intensified.

Lorne combatted the urge to shudder beneath his evil glare.

"No comment."

"Ah, but there was a reaction there, Mr. Platt. I'm right, aren't I? Everything would have been okay, and Mr. Lee would probably still be alive today if he hadn't snooped in that cupboard, yes?"

"No comment."

And that was how the rest of the interview panned out. As much as Lorne wanted to reach across the table and slap the suspect's face for frustrating the hell out of her, she didn't. "Okay, I'm happy to leave things there. I'll arrange your transport to the remand centre right away."

Mr. Jenson shuffled in his chair.

"Something wrong, Mr. Jenson?"

"No. So, my client has actually been arrested?"

"Were you not made aware of that upon your arrival? We don't usually interview suspects while they are wearing cuffs, Mr. Jenson."

"Yes, no, sorry."

Lorne and Sean glanced at each other in despair. Eager to move on to questioning Mrs. Platt, Lorne asked the uniformed police officer to take the prisoner back to his cell. "Bring in Mrs. Platt on your return. Thank you."

The officer helped Platt to his feet and guided him out of the room. Lorne ended the interview tape, ejected it from the machine, and wrote Platt's name and the case number on the tape. Then she glanced up at Jenson and said, "It would be helpful if you directed your next client to be compliant."

"Helpful for whom?"

The door opened, and in walked the cuffed Mrs. Platt, accompanied by a female officer, who steered the suspect to her seat. Jenson introduced himself to his client and leaned over to whisper something in her ear. Sean nudged Lorne with his leg, intimating he knew what the solicitor had just informed his client. Lorne suspected Sean was thinking along the same lines she was. She placed a new tape in the machine, switched it on, and again relayed the same information whilst smiling at the accused.

"Mrs. Platt, can you tell us when the renovation work started at your property?"

The woman stared long and hard at Lorne before she uttered the same words her infuriating husband had. "No comment."

"You've taught your client well, Mr. Jenson. Maybe you'd care to inform your client that the more she cooperates with us, the more lenient her sentence is likely to be in the long run."

"And you can guarantee that, Inspector, can you?" Jenson replied, curling his upper lip into a sickly smile.

"I can have a word in the right ear, if that's what you're asking? What's the alternative? Spending the rest of her life behind bars?"

Mrs. Platt looked sharply at Jenson. He gave her a warning look not to devour the carrot Lorne had dangled before her.

"Mrs. Platt, were you involved with the murders of the three tradesmen at your property?" Lorne asked quickly, while the woman's uncertainty was on show for all to see.

"No. I mean… no comment."

Lorne inhaled and exhaled a few short breaths before she asked, "What about the skeleton? How long has that been there?"

"No comment," Platt said, her eyes drifting down to the table.

"Who does the skeleton belong to, Mrs. Platt?"

"No comment."

"It's only a matter of time before we find out. I promise if you help us now, I'll put in more than a good word for you."

Mrs. Platt's gaze locked onto Lorne's again. "You would?"

"My client won't be led up the garden path, Inspector. Stop promising her things you have no control over. Be warned, your comments are on the tape, too."

"I'm well aware of that, Mr. Jenson. Mrs. Platt, why would you want to be locked up until the day you die if you're innocent of these crimes? Do you really love your husband that much? Is that love worth throwing the rest of your life away for?"

Mrs. Platt paused for a few seconds then said, "No comment."

"If that's all you have to say in response, then we might as well draw this interview to a close."

The woman let out a relieved sigh, but Lorne jumped on the chance to make her worried again.

"I have an appointment booked to visit your son. He seems very keen to tell us what he knows about this subject, and more, by all accounts."

The woman glared at Lorne through narrowed eyes. "He wouldn't dare. He knows nothing."

"Doesn't he? That's not what I picked up from the conversation we've already had. This is your last chance, Mrs. Platt. Are you going to work with us or not? The choice is yours."

The woman glanced at her solicitor once more as if in a genuine quandary about how to proceed for her own well-being. Another warning look from her solicitor appeared to help make up her mind. "No comment."

Lorne nodded, closed her notebook, and ended the tape. "You'll be transferred out of here to await your court appearance, where, no doubt, the judge will look badly on your lack of willingness to cooperate with this investigation. I sure hope you get accustomed to your prison cell quickly, Mrs. Platt. You'll be staring at the same bars for the rest of your life. How old are you now? Fifty? That's maybe thirty to forty years you'll have left to suffer in there. Do you think you're capable of surviving that?"

Mrs. Platt ignored Lorne's question and turned to Jenson. "I want to go back to my cell now."

"I'm sure the inspector can arrange that. I'll see you in court. You'll have the best barrister our firm can supply. I promise you."

"And how will your client be able to afford such a luxury, Mr. Jenson, if you don't mind me asking?"

"That's *our* business, Inspector, not yours."

Lorne watched the woman and her solicitor leave the room with the uniformed officer. "That sort of defence costs a lot of dosh. Nothing showed up in their bank accounts to indicate they have the sort of money to get them out of this mess."

"Perhaps they'll sell the house. Property prices in London have gone through the roof lately. That would be my guess anyway."

"We need to get Patti to rush the examination of the cellar, though, just in case the Platts get hauled up in front of the judge soon."

Sean nodded. "Agreed. Why don't we call it a day today?" He glanced down at his watch. "It's almost seven thirty now, and we'll start afresh tomorrow."

Lorne rubbed her forehead between her eyes. "Sounds like a good idea."

* * *

Denis cried out and woke up to find Sam leaning over him, smoothing the damp hair away from his brow.

"Sweetheart, you were dreaming, crying out in your sleep."

He wrapped his arms around her, pulling her close to him, and sobbed openly for the first time in years, relieved that his parents were behind bars, unable to hurt anyone else.

"Sweetheart, what's wrong? Is it because of the children? They'll be fine. I'm sure Inspector Warner will do her best to help us get them."

Denis remained silent, unsure whether to reveal his dark secret to Sam or not. Such an occasion had never risen before in their relationship. The guilt at hiding the truth from her was ripping his insides to shreds. He listened to her soothing words, entwined in her arms, the warmth of her body overcoming the cold sweat layering his tortured skin. Finally, he drifted off to sleep without uttering a single word. He would have to tell her one day. He had a feeling that day was just around the corner, too. The question was, whether he would survive the trauma of other people learning about his twisted past.

CHAPTER FIFTEEN

Questions bombarded her mind all night long. Finally, at five thirty, Lorne carefully got out of bed, hoping not to wake her sleeping husband, and went downstairs. After making a cup of coffee, she opened the back door and walked across the drive to the freshly dug mound of dirt. "Hello, boy." Tears filled her eyes the moment Henry's face filtered into her mind. A lump the size of an orange lodged in her throat, preventing her from saying more. Caring owners always found it hard to lose their beloved pets, but Henry had been so much more than a pet to her. He had been a constant companion that had seen her through some extremely rough times over the years, and she felt truly empty without him.

A hand gently touched her shoulder. "Mum? Are you all right?"

With tears streaming down her face, Lorne gathered her daughter in her arms and kissed the top of her head. "I will be, one day. It's still very raw. That's all, sweetie."

"I know, Mum. I still cry myself to sleep at night. I know we've opened our hearts to Sheba now, but she'll never take Henry's place. No dog could ever do that."

Lorne pushed Charlie away from her then wiped the tears from her eyes with her thumbs. "I'm so proud of you, Charlie. I don't say it nearly enough."

"You don't have to say it, Mum—I know. I'm proud of you, too. I always have been. One day, when I'm not so involved in this place, I'd still like to follow in your footsteps and become a copper."

Lorne's eyes widened in surprise. "Really? I thought you'd bypassed that plan when you took over here. I'm not sure how I feel about that, love. Criminals are getting harder to catch and using more and more dangerous ways to commit their crimes. There is one thing in our favour now, though…"

Charlie tilted her head. "What's that, Mum?"

"You know I've been supporting that coppers in the UK should be armed? Well, I'm going to get my chance soon enough."

"You're going to carry a gun?" Charlie asked, shocked.

"Not quite that far. I'm going to have Taser training, starting next week. Hey, it looks like we've just wrapped up another case, so there shouldn't be anything standing in the way of my proposed training."

"Wowza! Aren't those things supposed to be dangerous?"

"If used incorrectly, any weapon can be deadly in the wrong hands, Charlie. I think the aim is to use the Tasers more as a deterrent than to actually fire the damn things. The latest statistics seem to back that up, too. Most criminals are giving themselves up once the officers draw their Tasers out, ready to use."

Charlie shuddered. "I'm not surprised. I wouldn't fancy having fifty thousand volts going through me like that."

"You're well-informed on the subject. How did you know how many thousand volts it discharges?"

"I can't remember. I think I heard it recently on one of the forensic shows or something like that. How do you feel about being in charge of a Taser?"

"I'm not sure really. I've supported the right to carry guns for years. I suppose I have to feel a little responsible for Tasers coming into circulation. Apparently, thirty thousand officers have been authorised to use them at a cost of eight million pounds. It would be foolish to turn the opportunity down now."

"Good luck with the training. Let me know how it works out. Right, I have dogs to feed and exercise." She kissed Lorne on the cheek and hugged her. "Chin up, Mum."

"I'll get there, sweetie."

Lorne went back inside the house to get ready for work. She cooked a full English breakfast for Charlie and Tony then drove to the station early that morning. When she arrived, AJ was at his desk, as usual. "Are you sleeping here at the moment, young man?"

He laughed. "Not exactly, Lorne. I might as well be here rather than sitting in an empty flat."

"Have you heard from Katy? I should have rung her last night, but I was too exhausted when I got home. It's no excuse; I know."

"She understands that, Lorne. The doctor gave her some hopeful news yesterday. They're going to put her father on a revolutionary drug they're trialling that is supposed to repair the damage to his heart."

"Okay. How does Katy feel about that?"

He hitched up a shoulder. "Anything is better than nothing at this point. He's not responded to any other treatment they've tried, so why not?"

"Not sure how I'd feel if they told me my father was going to be a pioneering guinea pig."

"I hear you. Looking at it the other way—they've tried everything else except a heart transplant, so what choice do they have?"

"Still a tough decision to make. Is her mum holding up okay?"

"She appears to be. She's grateful that Katy is there with her to deal with the doctors *et cetera.*"

"At times like this, families should always stick together and support each other." Lorne mentally kicked herself for not ringing her sister, Jade, lately, and she promised herself to do that either during the week or at the weekend when Charlie was away.

"I agree. What's on the agenda today, now that we've caught the criminals?"

The phone on Lorne's desk rang, and she rushed to answer it. "Hello, DS Warner," she said, hastily forgetting her new title.

"It's the desk sergeant, ma'am. I suppose I better ask if you're sitting down?"

"Get on with it, Sergeant?"

"Ma'am, we've been told that Courtney Platt has escaped."

"My God! This is a sick joke, isn't it?" She glanced over at AJ, her free arm slapping her thigh out of despair.

"No, ma'am. The reports are that the van hit another vehicle and ended up in the hedgerow. They're blaming it on the fog we had last night."

"Sod the weather report. What the effing hell is being done to catch the bastard?" Lorne collapsed into her chair. AJ left his desk and sat in the spare chair opposite her. Lorne covered the phone and filled him in on the drama. "Platt has gone missing."

"Shit!" AJ responded.

The desk sergeant calling said that an alert had been issued immediately, but nothing had materialised regarding the escaped convict as yet.

"What a bloody mess. When did this happen?"

"Um… at eleven last night, ma'am."

"What? And I'm just learning about this now because?"

"I don't know, ma'am. I've not long come on duty myself."

"Okay, we're wasting time, and I have a dangerous bloody criminal to catch. Where did the accident happen?"

The sergeant gave Lorne the location. She jotted it down then slammed the phone into the cradle. "Pull up a map, AJ. Let's see if we can work out where he's heading."

They both rushed to AJ's computer screen. "It's in the middle of nowhere, in the midst of a forest, Lorne."

"Shit and double shit. I better let the chief know." Lorne pulled out her mobile, aware that Sean wouldn't be at work yet, and rang his mobile. "Sean, it's Lorne. Platt's escaped."

"He's *what*? Jesus, when?"

"I'm bloody furious. It happened at eleven o'clock last night, and I've just found out. AJ and I have located the area on the map. It's thick forest. We'll never catch the bastard."

"Okay, I'm ten minutes from the station. Let me pull in some favours when I get there. We can organise a search team. He won't get away from us, Lorne. Get onto the ports *et cetera.*"

"On my to-do list. Can we go to the scene ourselves first thing?"

"Of course. I'll see you soon—and Lorne?"

"Yes?"

"Don't worry. We'll catch him. He can't have gone far."

Lorne disconnected the call and shook her head. Then an idea struck her. She grabbed her mobile again and dialled a number she obtained from flicking through her notebook. "Hi, Denis. This is Lorne Warner."

"Hello, Lorne. Are you ringing to tell me social services have changed their mind?"

"No. I'm sorry. I'll get onto that later on today. Denis, I have some bad news for you."

She heard the man humph as if he'd dropped into a chair. "Go on."

"It's your father. He's escaped. I wanted to warn you in case he turns up there."

"Fuck! How did this happen?"

"There was an accident. I need to get on and try to find him but wanted you to be aware of the situation first. Do you have any idea where he would go, Denis?"

Denis exhaled. "I can't think of anywhere. Not off the top of my head. Can I have a think about it and get back to you, Lorne?"

"Sure. We need to act swiftly, Denis. Try to think of places you went during your childhood—a favourite holiday spot, anything along those lines."

The man stayed silent, then said, "Nothing is coming to mind right now. I'll think about it and call you if I remember anything. Please, hurry up and find him. There's every chance he could come after me."

Baffled, Lorne asked, "Why, Denis?"

"Just take my word for it, Lorne. I'll get back to you soon."

"Denis, before you go, I'll organise a squad car to sit outside your property. Will that help?"

"Thank you. I appreciate that."

Lorne spent the next ten minutes making a series of urgent calls whilst tugging her hair from its roots during some of them. Sean barged through the incident room doors as she was hanging up from her final call.

"Any news?"

"Not yet. I've rung Denis to warn him, just in case his father decides to show up there."

"You've alerted the ports and airports?"

"Yep. Did you manage to call in any favours?" Lorne asked.

"Not yet. All my contact details are at my desk. I'll get on it straight away. Let's hit this hard and fast for the next half an hour. It's not too late. If he's still in the vicinity, we can pick him up before he has a chance to get too far away."

Lorne shook her head. "We're talking ten hours since the incident occurred, Sean. I very much doubt that he'll still be in the area. I'm going to get the dog tracking team out there. Hopefully, they'll pick up a scent at least."

"Good idea. Let me get onto my contacts. I'll be right back."

True to his word, Sean pulled a few strings and arranged several teams to join them at the scene of the accident. Lorne got out of the car and ran to inspect the van for herself. She walked all around it, trying to find any clues as to why the vehicle left the road. It wasn't until she reached the back of the van that she noticed a dent in the bumper. She pointed out the twisted metal to Sean. "I wonder if that was there before the accident. I need to find out what has happened to the police driver, too."

Sean took out his phone and made a call to the station to ask if the vehicle had any damage to its rear before it was used to transport the prisoner. He shook his head at Lorne and hung up. "Nope, it was in good nick. You're thinking this was no accident?"

"Yep. What if there's a third person involved in this that we know nothing about? What if they took the risk and forced the vehicle off the road to help him escape?" Lorne looked over her shoulder and saw one of the police dog handlers at the rear of his vehicle unloading one of his dogs. "Hey, over here," she called.

The officer and his German shepherd dog trotted across the road to join them.

"Hi, I'm Acting Detective Inspector Warner. Can you try and pick up the suspect's scent from here? I want to know if he set off into the woods on foot or if there was another car waiting for him."

While the officer and the dog worked the area, Lorne again cursed herself for calling Denis. *What if he's involved? What if he's the third person? I've just warned him that we're aware of his dad's escape! Shit! Me and my big mouth.* But then her other inner voice reprimanded her and told her she'd done the right thing by ringing Denis. That voice was absolutely adamant that Denis was innocent.

Sean nudged her elbow and asked, "What are you thinking?"

"Where, why, who... you know, the usual stuff. You don't suppose the son was part of this elaborate plan, do you?"

"I wouldn't like to say. You're the one who usually has a sixth sense about folks."

"Yeah, I know at this moment in time, my inner voice is having an almighty argument with itself. No!" she stated definitively. "It can't be him. I'm going to ring AJ, get him to do further checks, see if there's another member of the family that has escaped our radar so far." Lorne took a few steps then pulled her mobile from her jacket pocket. "AJ, it's me. Do me a favour and start delving into the family tree. See if we've missed out a relative who could have been involved in the murders and helped Platt escape."

"Right. So you don't think it was just an accident then, boss?"

"No. The rear bumper has evidence of being struck. Can you also check if Mrs. Platt made it to the remand centre?"

"I'll get on it right away. Hopefully, get back to you soon."

"Wait, AJ! Can you also find out where the driver is? If he's in a hospital, which one? When you find out, ask either Stephen or Graham to chase it up, see if the driver has made a statement of the events. If he hasn't, get one."

"Will do."

Lorne ended the call. She rejoined Sean and the dog handler. "Anything?"

"Yes, the scent disappeared about here." He pointed to a spot in the middle of the road.

"So, it's as we expected. He had a bloody accomplice."

"Looks that way. We might as well call off the search of the area in that case. We can utilise the men to form a wider search, yes?" Sean asked.

"Agreed. We need to go and see Denis, I think."

"As a suspect?" Sean asked, raising an eyebrow.

"No, not really. For information about where his father is likely to head for. I asked him on the phone earlier, but he couldn't think of anywhere. I'm not happy about leaving it there, though. We should show up in person, see if the pressure of seeing us jolts a memory or something."

They pulled up outside Denis and Sam's flat. Lorne nodded to the uniformed officer sitting in his squad car across the road from the flat. Sam opened the door the second the bell rang. She seemed upset and jittery.

"Is Denis in, Sam?"

"He is. Can I have a word before you see him?"

"Of course. About what?" Lorne replied, glancing sideways at Sean.

Sam pulled the front door closed behind her and spoke quietly, "I'm worried about him. He woke me up during the night, crying out."

"What exactly is bothering him? Do you know?"

Sam breathed in deeply before she answered, "I think it's the kids. He needs the children to be here with him."

"I've already told him that I'm trying my best, Sam. These things take time to sort out, and if he isn't on the foster carers list, honestly, I don't think there's much chance of the kids being allowed to stay here."

"I understand that, Lorne. Nonetheless, he's cared for those kids for months now. Taking them away from him is destroying him."

"I have to ask one question, Sam. Do you believe the children have been abused by Denis's parents?"

Sam gasped and shook her head, her expression full of uncertainty. "I have no idea. The family are very secretive. Even Denis doesn't talk much about his parents. Goodness, is that what you really believe?"

"It's pure speculation for now, Sam. Have the kids ever mentioned anything when they've stayed here?"

"No. Denis goes out of his way to make them happy when they stay with us. He loves them to pieces, Lorne."

"You must have visited the kids at the Platts' home. Have you ever noticed a difference in their behaviour?" Lorne asked.

"Not really, not that I've visited them much there. Denis's parents don't take kindly to visitors. At least that's what I've gathered. Of course, it might just be me they object to visiting their home."

"Why? Have you done anything to upset them in the past?"

"Not that I know of. Denis has always reassured me that they can be funny buggers with strangers. That's when I started to limit my visits to see them, not that Denis goes there much, either. He only really visits when he's either picking up or dropping off the children."

Lorne nodded. "When the kids are here, do they ever say what it's like living at home?"

"Not really. To be honest, sometimes when they come, they can be very reserved, quiet, not wanting to laugh, as though they have the horrendous weight of the world on their shoulders. I leave Denis to chat to them for a while, and then they seem fine."

"What about when it's time for them to return home? What's their reaction like then, Sam?"

"Hit and miss. I tend to leave their care to Denis most of the times. He has a special way with kids, any kids. He seems to be like a magnet to most of them. Even strangers' kids are drawn to him in the street."

"That's unusual, and you've never thought how strange that is?"

Sam frowned. "No, the thought has never crossed my mind. Why should it? What are you getting at, Lorne?"

"Nothing really. Nothing derogatory anyway. Sorry if it came across that way. Can we see him now? Just one thing before we go up—has Denis told you what happened last night?"

"No! What?"

"His father has escaped. The van he was being transported to the remand centre in crashed, and he got away. We think he had help. Any idea who would want to risk their necks doing such a thing, Sam?"

She shook her head. "No, should I? Hang on. Are you saying that Denis helped his dad? There's no way on earth he would ever contemplate doing that."

"Where was Denis last night?"

"Here with me, *all* night, Inspector. He never left the flat, not for a second."

"Good, and you'd be willing to give us a statement to that effect should we need one?"

"Of course."

Denis's forearms were resting on his thighs, and his hands were clenched together, trembling, when Lorne and Sam walked into the lounge.

"Hello, Denis. No, stay there," Lorne said as Denis attempted to stand. She crossed the room and sat on the sofa next to him. "Are you all right?"

He shook his head. His gaze remained fixed on the rug in front of the gas fire. "Would you be? Knowing that your father, a man on remand for several murders, is on the loose, and likely to show up at your door any minute?"

"I'm sorry. It was a dumb question, Denis. Forgive me." Lorne continued, "Is that all that is bothering you? Not meaning to sound flippant, or is there something else you're not telling us about?"

Denis's gaze located Sam.

She nodded and smiled at him. "Trust her, Denis. Lorne is on your side, sweetheart."

Denis turned to look at Lorne, his eyes glassy with threatening tears. "It's difficult to talk about this after I've buried it so deep for many years."

"Try. We're not going to judge you. I promise." Lorne looked at Sean and Sam, who both nodded at her. Lorne placed a comforting hand lightly on Denis's clenched hands, trying to calm the trembling, which appeared to have increased.

"Images keep jumping into my head. Vile, disturbing images that I need to figure out, put into some kind of order."

"From your childhood, Denis? Is that what you're referring to?"

He nodded slowly. "Yes." Then Denis looked up at Sam. "I'm sorry, darling."

Sam rushed across the room and knelt in front of him. "For what? Denis, you're the most compassionate human being I've ever come across. You have *nothing* to be sorry about. If you can tell us what you know, I'll support you from this day forward without any recriminations. I love you for the person you are now, not for what you have been in the past. Do you hear me, Denis?" Sam kissed the tip of his nose.

Even Lorne had to swipe her hand across her eyes at the outpouring of love she was witnessing between the couple. She remained silent, as they all did, until Denis was ready to open up to them.

Denis sniffed and shook his head. His gaze glued to the rug once more, he seemed to contemplate what to say next. They waited and waited until finally, he broke the silence, not even trying to stem the flow of tears that accompanied his speech. "They abused me. They abused all of us at one time or another."

Lorne's hand tightened around his, and a large lump lodged itself in her neck. "Both of them, Denis? Your mother and your father, they both abused you?"

His head bounced up and down constantly. His breath came in short, sharp gasps at the same time. "Yes, and others."

"Other children, is that what you mean? Or other adults, Denis?" Lorne probed gently.

"All the children." He paused, sucked in a shuddering breath, then continued, "And every adult that entered the home abused us, too."

Lorne's heart rate increased. She glanced at Sean and Sam. Each of them had either tears rolling down their face or moist eyes. Only a person without compassion wouldn't have been affected by his words. "Did you ever seek help, Denis?"

He shook his head. "Some of the teachers and social workers were in on it."

"What? Are you telling me that the very people entrusted to care for you, abused you also?"

"Yes."

"I'm so sorry. No child should ever be subjected to what you've had to deal with, no child." The image of Charlie being raped by the Unicorn flashed through Lorne's mind. She shook her head to dislodge the vile image and concentrated all her energy on learning the truth about what had taken place in this man's parents' house of horrors.

"In the cellar, we found a skeleton. Any idea who that could belong to, Denis?"

He turned to look at Lorne. "No. Was it a child's skeleton?"

"I have no idea right now. The forensic team are at the house, conducting their examination of the scene. Do you have any indication what your parents intended doing in the cellar? Why they've been renovating the area?"

"No, no idea. Growing up, we were forbidden to go down there. One of the boys went down there once, and he was whipped daily for a whole week, spent the week in his room without food. Only one glass of water passed his lips a day." He gripped either side of his head and began rocking back and forth on the edge of the sofa. "I can still hear his screams. Why? Why did they do that to an innocent boy? Why were they allowed to treat us the way they did, are doing?"

"Are you saying this type of abuse has been going on with the kids in their care today, Denis?"

"Yes. They come here for a respite from the abuse. I know what they're going through and wanted to show them that true love really exists, what *love* is really like. Both Sam and I are guilty of spoiling them when they are here."

"Why? Sorry, I mean, why do your parents allow the kids to visit here? Were you allowed to leave the house when you were being abused?"

"No. I can't tell you the reason why. Maybe it's because my parents are older now. I'm grasping at straws with that, not knowing what else to say. They have never given me a reason, just told me to take them for a few days."

"Have they only asked you to look after the children recently, Denis, while the work has been going on at the house or what?"

"The past few months, I suppose. Since they've had Emily, Colette, and Dwain. I'm not sure how long the work has been in progress, though."

"It does seem strange, doesn't it?" Lorne glanced up at Sean.

He nodded and prodded his head.

"What is it, boss?"

"Maybe it coincides with the times when they killed the tradesmen. Perhaps they didn't want the kids around to see the murders."

"That seems plausible." She turned her attention back to Denis again. "I need to know if your parents could have an accomplice?

Someone helped your father to break free last night. We need to find out who that person is, Denis."

"My father had a half-brother who used to… visit the house years ago. I haven't seen or heard from him since I left home. I refused to have any contact with the bastard. He was one of the worst…"

"I'm sorry to push you on this, but any idea where he lives? Could your father be hiding out at his house?"

Denis shrugged. "I have no idea. He moves around a lot, from what I can recall. She'll know. You need to ask the woman who raised me."

"Your mum?" Lorne could totally understand him not wanting to call her such a privileged name, after all the mistreatment she had bestowed upon him over the years. The images he had been forced to return to had obviously pulled the hatred out from its hiding place.

"Yes. Don't let her get away with this, I beg of you. She was as much party to what she dished out in the form of punishment as he was. They were a team, a dangerous and perverse team."

"You have my assurance that they'll both get what is coming to them. Can you tell me this man's name, Denis?"

"He used to go under the name of Jim Porter. Once I heard my father call him by another surname. I think it was Collins."

"That's great, very helpful. And he lived in the London area? It would help us to track him down if we knew that."

"I think so. I repeat, he used to move around a lot."

"Don't worry. If he's out there, my team will find him. Look, you have my number. If you ever need to chat, just call me, no matter what time of day that might be. Promise me that? Sam is here for you, too. She loves you. Don't push her away. I've heard heinous crimes like this often have a better outcome, if the person dealing with the pain opens up to others. If you like, I can arrange some form of counselling to help you through this. I take it fear prevented you from contacting the police?"

"Yes. That and the kids said that my parents had threatened to kill them if they ever opened their mouths." He squeezed the bridge of his nose then continued, "Thank you. I appreciate your offer. Let's get my father picked up first, and then I'll decide what to do about this." He prodded his temple. "At the moment, the thought of that man being on the loose is far more disturbing than what has taken place in my past."

Lorne patted his hand. "We'll get him. On that, you have my word."

Sean stepped forward and rested a hand on Denis's shoulder. "And mine. We'll try to ease your pain, Denis. It won't be easy, but we'll do our best for you."

"Thank you. From me and on behalf of the other children they've hurt, too."

Sam saw them to the door because when Denis tried to stand up, his legs gave way beneath him, and he broke down and cried.

"Thanks, Sam. He's going to need you more now than ever before. Are you sure you're up to the challenge?"

"I'm sure. I love him, even more now. Promise me you'll string those bastards up?"

Lorne nodded. "I wish it were that simple to hang them, but the maximum they will get is life in a six-by-six cell. Go, we'll see ourselves out. Go and take care of Denis. Ring me if he remembers anything significant, like where his father might hide, or anything else for that matter. I'm here for both of you, okay?"

"Thank you."

Lorne shut the door to the flat behind them, then she and Sean walked to the car. Inside the car, she asked Sean to excuse her for a second or two as she broke down in tears herself. Sean put the car into gear and headed back to the station. Now and again, he rested a concerned hand on Lorne's thigh.

She blew her nose and smiled at him. "All better now, sorry. I had to get it out of my system. I'm going to make sure we capture that bastard soon. All I ask is that you allow me to spend five minutes alone with him."

"What good will that do, Lorne? If you attack him, it'll only go against you in court, jeopardise the case."

"It'll make me feel better at least. Okay, have it your way. But if the shit tries to resist arrest, I'll handle him, yes?"

"You have my word on that, Inspector."

CHAPTER SIXTEEN

The instant they pulled into the station car park, Lorne's mobile rang. "Hello?"

"Lorne, it's Patti. I think you need to get over here pronto."

"Where? At the Platts' house?"

"Yes, we're still here, and by the looks of things, we're going to be here for a long time to come yet."

"That sounds ominous. We're on our way. See you in fifteen minutes."

Lorne hung up and smiled tautly at Sean. "No rest for the wicked, eh?"

"Sounded serious. What's up?" Sean asked, turning the key in the ignition and setting off again.

"She didn't say. I suspect you're right, though."

Several forensic technicians were in the kitchen when Lorne and Sean arrived at the house. Each of them was holding a cup of coffee bought from a nearby Costa coffee shop.

Patti sighed wearily. "We're just taking five minutes before we start again."

"You don't have to justify your actions to us, Patti. You know that. Dare I ask what you've found?" Lorne replied, leaning against the doorframe of the kitchen.

"Bodies. Lots of them."

"What? How many are we talking about?"

Patti shrugged. "It's too early to tell. At the last count, we had five. Who's to say how many more are down there? For all we know, they could be buried on top of each other. Our equipment would only pick up the first body."

Patti led the way down into the cellar, with Lorne and Sean close behind her. She pointed to an area near the back of the cellar, where the forensic team's equipment was set up and several numbered markers dotted the floor. "Don't go any closer, not without a suit on."

"Holy shit. Have you only detected the bodies, or have you actually dug any up yet? Sorry, I'm trying to ascertain what condition the corpses are in and how long they've been down there."

"I think it's safe to assume the bodies will be all skeletal remains, judging by what we found in the cupboard."

"Why? Why place that one body in the cupboard yet bury all the others?" Sean asked over Lorne's shoulder.

"Good question, and one that will need hours of examinations to obtain the answers, Chief," Patti replied, shaking her head at the daunting prospect that lay ahead of her.

"Christ, it's even more imperative to track the bastard down now."

"Wait! What do you mean, Lorne?" Patti asked.

Lorne shrugged. "The fucker has escaped."

"Shit! When?" Patti asked, shaking her head.

"Don't concern yourself with that. We have loads of teams on the lookout for the bastard. We should get back to the station. Is there anything else you can tell us, Patti, before we shoot off?"

"Nope, I just wanted you to know what we'd found. I suspect we'll find a lot more once we rip this place apart. There's no way we can leave this with just digging up the cellar. Who knows what we'll find behind all the walls? I worked a case a few years back, where a man and his wife set up a brothel in their home and killed all the customers. You should have seen how many bodies were squeezed under the floorboards and in the walls of that place! And that was a one-bedroomed flat."

Lorne sighed heavily. "This is going to take an eternity to go over. Can you call in more teams?"

"Like you, we're under restrictions, but I'm sure they'll make an exception here. I'll make the call anyway and see. You two go. There's little you can do here. Good luck in your hunt for him. I'll check in with you in a day or two, let you know how things are progressing."

"Thanks, Patti."

Lorne and Sean left the house and jumped back in the car.

"That's going to be so time-consuming, more like an archaeological dig than a crime scene," Sean suggested, fisting the steering wheel.

"I'd say you were spot on with that assumption. Jesus, Sean, how the fuck are we going to track this bastard down? We have to pull out all the stops on this one, don't we?"

"It certainly looks that way."

Their second attempt to park up and enter the station was a successful one. At the top of the stairs, Lorne and Sean temporarily parted ways. "Listen up, people," she called out as she pushed through the swing doors to the incident room. "We've just come back from the Platts' house. The forensic team have discovered multiple bodies buried in the cellar. We're not sure how many as yet. Suffice it to say, we need to put everything into finding this monster Platt."

The team murmured their distaste at what Lorne had shared.

"The chief has gone to have a word with the superintendent to see if he can get us more men on this case. After all, we've got a serial killer with a high body count on the loose. Stephen, did you manage to see the driver at the hospital?"

"Yes, ma'am. They roughed him up pretty good. Saying that, it sounds like he was lucky compared to the others who have crossed Platt's path."

"Indeed. Could he tell you anything about what happened?"

"In between bouts of coughing up blood, he told me the make of the car—a dark old-type Merc. Unfortunately, he didn't get a chance to make out the registration number."

"Okay. Well, we have a couple of names to run through the system. Maybe we can match something up. Is the driver going to recover from the attack?"

"In time. Might take a few months of bed rest, the doc said."

Lorne's eyes narrowed as she thought about what she wanted to do in retaliation to Platt and his associate. "AJ, get me all you can on Jim Porter or Jim Collins. According to Denis Platt, this man used to frequent the house often and is the most likely candidate to be the one Courtney Platt would turn to in times of trouble."

"On it right away." AJ's fingers danced across his keyboard.

Lorne walked up to the whiteboard and noted down the man's name, his alias, and the make of the car that had caused the driver to end up in a ditch. Then she debated whether she should ring Denis and Sam, to update them on what the team had discovered at the house, but she quickly reconsidered. Instead, she rang Ms. Murray at social services to give the woman a piece of her mind.

"Yes, Ms. Murray? It's Acting Detective Inspector Lorne Warner here."

"Detective, I'm extremely…"

"Busy? Yes, aren't we all? Let's get one thing straight from the get-go shall we, Ms. Murray? You *will* from now on take my calls seriously, or I will do my damnedest to get you fired. Am I making myself perfectly clear?"

The woman gasped. "Really, Inspector! What gives you the right to talk to me in such an aggressive tone?"

"For a start, the checks you've been making on the children in the Platts' care are nothing short of laughable. You should be shot for even placing those vulnerable babies with such bloody monsters."

"Now wait just a minute. Why on earth are you calling them monsters? What proof do you have that they're not upstanding citizens in the community?"

"If you let me *finish,* I'll tell you!" The rest of the team stared at Lorne. She motioned for them to get on with their work. "Actually, I'm going to send a member of my team over to interview you under caution."

"What? Why?"

"Because, to be honest, from what I've heard today, I have every reason to believe you're probably in on the scam." Lorne bit her lip. She realised she'd gone too far, but her buttons had been pushed too many times over the last few days for her to care what the consequences to her actions might be. She had no intention of backing off.

"What the bloody hell are you talking about? I demand to speak to your superior officer. You're mad woman."

"Are you telling me you had no idea that the Platts are serial killers?"

"What a bloody absurd question. You're really expecting me to answer such nonsense? I suggest you speak to my supervisor before you start flinging accusations in my direction, Detective. I've never heard such tripe in all my years in the service."

"Maybe I've said too much already. Yes, you better put me on to your supervisor, and I'm warning you, Ms. Murray, don't even consider leaving town until this case has been solved. I will be sending over a member of my team this afternoon to take down your statement."

"Do what you wish, Detective. What you have told me is complete news to me. Why the devil you should think I'm involved in this 'scam,' as you put it, is far beyond my comprehension. At the moment, I feel sick to my stomach for you thinking such a heinous thing of me."

Lorne cringed. Maybe her judgement of the woman had been clouded by what Denis had said about her predecessors. "Okay, you better pass me over to your supervisor then." Lorne was not in the mood to issue an apology to the obnoxious woman just yet.

She heard the phone hit the desk, and she waited. Then someone picked up the phone, and the call was patched through to another extension.

"Hello, Inspector Warner. This is Karen Harborn. I'm the supervisor in charge today. Why are you going around accusing my staff of not fulfilling their duties properly?"

"Hello, Karen. Right, let me say this to begin with, I don't want to start off on the wrong foot with you here, but I need to get Ms. Murray taken off duty until this case is solved."

"I'm afraid you don't have the authority to make such a request. Please give me your reasons?"

Lorne ran through what had happened between her and Murray over the last few days first and then hit the supervisor with the biggie. "It has come to our attention today that the Platts are serial killers. Unless you make a habit of placing foster children in these types of homes, I'm suggesting that you look further into Ms. Murray's background before letting her continue in her role, as we have a witness who is willing to give us a statement, saying that social services knew and even assisted in the crimes."

"That's appalling. How on earth was Ms. Murray to know that the couple were or are serial killers? As for the second point you've raised, that will have to be taken up with my superiors."

"Don't worry, I will. I have no intention of letting this matter drop, I assure you. Regarding Ms. Murray, one visit from me, and I was able to smell a rat with the couple. How many foster homes in your region are spotless when there are three children in residence?"

"That's a very illogical question, Inspector. I'm not entirely sure I understand what you're getting at."

"Maybe it's my detective skills coming in to play in this instance then, but I was more than a little confused when I visited the Platts recently and found that there wasn't a single toy anywhere to be seen in that house, neither downstairs in the lounge nor in the kiddies' bedrooms. Wouldn't that strike you as strange, Karen?"

"I suppose if you put it like that, yes. How is that Ms. Murray's fault, though, Inspector?"

"Well, if anything comes across as being odd on her visits, shouldn't that be noted down on the couple's file? To me, it sounds suspiciously like a cover-up."

"Yes, ordinarily, it is. I'll look into it. Is there anything else?"

"Yes. I'm requesting that I have access to the Platts' fostering records."

"I think you'll need some form of paperwork before I hand that kind of information over, Inspector, if we're going to do things by the book."

Lorne exhaled loudly. "Even though I've laid it on the table that we're looking at a couple of serial killers here? I can get a warrant, but that is going to take time, Karen."

"That's the way it has to be, Inspector. From our point of view, there are no longer children at risk staying with the couple. Our job is done. What are you hoping to find in the files, if you don't mind me asking?"

"Probably nothing, given what the son of the couple told us today about a cover-up, but it is imperative that I know how many children stayed at the residence over the years. I really can't go into further detail about that side of things right now. I'd hate for something to be leaked to the press while there is an escaped convict on the run. That'll be Mr. Platt, whom your department has apparently thought very highly of over the years."

"Sarcasm doesn't become you, Inspector. I'm willing to let that remark slip by, allowing for the stress you are under at the present. Get me your warrant, and I'll send the files over for your perusal immediately. Good day, Inspector."

The woman hung up, leaving a seething Lorne taking out her frustration on the chair beside her. "Ugh... some people get right on my tits at times."

"Lorne, is something wrong?" Superintendent Anne White asked when she walked into the room with an embarrassed Sean standing alongside her.

"Sorry, ma'am. Damn paper-pushers standing in our way, as usual."

Anne tilted her head. "Who? I'll have a word. You shouldn't be caught up in menial tasks like this. You and the chief should be out there, searching for this killer."

"It's all right, ma'am. I'll get AJ to chase up the warrant I need for gaining access to the Platts' foster files."

The super nodded. "You think some of the bodies the pathologist has discovered could belong to some of the children in their care?"

"Yes, ma'am. It's a total mess. I've heard about so many of these bloody cases lately. Children of all ages being abused by people in authority—the very people who should have their care uppermost in their minds. I never thought in a million years that I'd end up with such a case on my patch. It sickens and saddens me, bloody paedophile rings."

Anne approached Lorne's desk and gripped her shoulder. Lowering her voice she said, "Lorne, I completely understand what this is doing to you as a mother. What I need you to do is cast those feelings aside for a while and start thinking as a DI. Turn the disgust into anger and get out there and bring this bastard to justice. You can do it. I have every faith in you."

"Yes, ma'am. I'm trying. I assure you. But where little kids are concerned and I hear that people have abused the system in order to terrorise innocent children... aggghhh! Okay, I'm all better now."

Anne winked at her. "That's my girl. Now, I've been on the phone to the commissioner and have arranged for the surrounding police forces to pitch in and lend us a hand. It's imperative that we capture this man ASAP, agreed?"

"Yes, ma'am." She craned her neck around the super and called out, "AJ? Any news on that vehicle or address yet?"

"Would you believe the system is playing up? I'm trying different ways to get the info, boss. Bear with me."

"Quick as you can, AJ."

"What about the son? Has he assisted you at all? Does he know anything about what was going on in that house?" the super asked.

"To be honest, I think he's suppressed the memories. And who could blame him? I'm going easy on him for the time being. He's scared shitless that his father is on the run."

"Does he think he'll turn up at his house?"

"I think so. Although, I have my doubts. I've arranged for a squad car to sit outside the house just in case."

"As a deterrent. Good idea—"

AJ erupted, "I've got it. Porter's address, I mean."

"Excuse me, ma'am." Lorne leapt out of her chair and grabbed the piece of paper AJ was waving excitedly at her.

Lorne gave the super an apologetic look and glanced in Sean's direction.

"Go!" the super shouted at them. "And don't return without them, either of them. That's an order," she shouted, wagging her finger.

Sean ran ahead of Lorne down the stairs and called over his shoulder, "No pressure there then!"

"She wants him off the streets as much as we do, Sean. I have one regret about this."

Sean paused and turned to look at her. "What's that?"

"That I haven't had my Taser training yet. I'd love to zap the little fucker with fifty thousand volts."

Sean continued down the stairs two at a time, laughing and shaking his head, which made her laugh, too.

They pulled up at the rundown address, which was situated in the shittiest road in the area. An unsettling feeling squeezed Lorne's stomach muscles; she suspected they were wasting their time.

"No car of that description around here," Lorne said.

"No garage, either. Let's knock on the door anyway."

"You knock. I'll scoot around the back just in case." A few steps into the trash-filled alleyway made Lorne regret her decision. She squeezed past a sodden stained mattress and the ripped easy chair blocking her way. Then she counted the houses to make sure she was heading for the right one. Looking up at the second floor window, she saw no sign of life inside. She eased open the gate, which teetered on one hinge, and covered her nose and mouth with her hand at the unbearable stench that greeted her. *Disgusting pigs! No, I take that back. Pigs are far cleaner than this mob.*

She placed her other hand up against the kitchen window and reeled back at the state the occupants had left the kitchen in. How long the pile of dishes had been sitting in the sink like that was anybody's guess. The question was if any of the mess had been freshly made. Lorne scanned the top plates and came to the conclusion that the stains on the green plates were anything but fresh, more than likely a few days old. She doubted the men had visited the address for at least forty-eight hours. After picking her way gingerly back through the debris-filled garden and alley, Lorne found Sean coming away from the front door.

"Nothing. You?" Sean asked.

"Negative. Is it worth asking the neighbours?"

"I doubt it. Seems like an area where people keep their noses to themselves or risk being done over."

"That's true enough. What now?" Lorne asked, casting her eyes first one way up the street then the other.

"Jump in. We'll think about that in the car."

Sean drove around the area a few times, searching for the suspect's car, but it proved to be a pointless exercise.

Lorne's mobile rang. "Hi, AJ. What have you got for us?"

"First, I wanted to tell you that the warrant you requested to obtain the paperwork from social services, will be available later this afternoon."

"Brilliant news. What else?"

"We're getting sightings coming in about the car."

"Where?" Lorne put her thumb up to Sean. He pulled the car over as she continued her conversation with AJ.

"Heading down to Brighton."

"Shit! We'll get after it. Patch through the route it's taking to my mobile when you receive further reports, AJ. Okay?"

"Will do, boss."

Lorne hung up and mulled things over for a moment.

Sean nudged her with his elbow and put the car in motion again. "What are you thinking?"

Lorne sucked in the air between her teeth. "Whether I should ring Denis or not."

"Why?"

"If I tell him their location, it might jolt a memory of a place they used to visit in the area during his childhood."

"Okay. Why the doubt?"

"What if he informs them we're closing in on them?"

Sean indicated and filtered into the traffic on the main road. "Listen, I got the impression that he's totally shaken up about this. I didn't pick up any vibes that he shouldn't be trusted, but if you have doubts about that, then you need to trust your instincts."

"To be honest with you, Sean, I've never been so confused about a person. Logically, I'm thinking the guy is a mess with reason, but then I'm thinking if my parents had abused me like that, would I still be in contact with them today? The answer categorically would be no."

"I hear you on that, Lorne. I'd feel the same way. However, put yourself in his shoes. Knowing that your mother and father are still fostering kids, wouldn't you do everything you could to save those kids?"

"Granted. So why hasn't he dobbed his parents in to the authorities? Or better still, run off with the kids? That would be my first choice."

Sean nodded as he thought of a response to her dilemma. "But then, to be fair, he has been letting the kids stay with him and Sam. Maybe that was his way of helping them, giving them a few days respite from the abuse."

"All right, taking that on board, would you be willing to hand those kids back after their stay with you?"

"No. But again, who knows how people's minds work in such circumstances?"

She sighed wearily. "Decisions, decisions. I need someone to guide me." Lorne clicked her fingers and rang Carol. "Hi, love. It's me. How are you feeling?"

"Sometimes good and at other times, not so good. What can I do for you, Lorne?"

"Sorry to hear that. I need your advice. I'm in a quandary what to do for the best, Carol."

"I'm rusty at the moment. Hang on. Let me see what I can come up with." Carol started humming, and Lorne imagined her rocking back and forth in her chair as she tapped into her spirit guide. "Sorry, Lorne. I can't add to what I told you the other day."

"That's too bad, hon. I know I don't usually give you any hints, but we've had a call that the car we're after is on its way to Brighton. Does that help?"

Carol inhaled and exhaled a few times then said vaguely, "A cottage. I can't tell you any more than that. Sorry, love."

"That will have to do, Carol. Don't beat yourself up about it. I'm sure what you've already given us has and will come in handy in the future. Take care. Ring you soon." Lorne disconnected the call and threw her mobile into her lap.

"The one time you really need your friend to come through, eh?"

"Yeah, she's gutted about it. She mentioned a cottage, though. Sod it! I'm going to ring Denis."

Sean nodded. "Wisest idea you've had all day."

"Denis, hi. Sorry to disturb you. It's Lorne."

"Hello, Lorne. I was just looking up your phone number to give you a call."

"You were. About what?"

"An image I unlocked in my head. I need to get in the house. Is that possible?"

"Ordinarily, I'd say no. You're not supposed to go near the place while the forensic team are there. What's it concerning, Denis?"

"The attic. I need to get in the attic."

"Crap. Okay. But not unless I'm there with you. Have you got that?"

"Of course. It can wait. I'll concentrate hard on conjuring up more suppressed memories in the meantime."

"Good. While you're at it, I need you to do more thinking for me."

"Oh?"

"The reason I'm ringing is because we have news regarding your father's whereabouts."

Denis gasped. "You've found him?"

"Not yet. We've had notification that this Porter fella's car has been spotted near Brighton. I wondered if you could really dig deep and tell me where he's likely to be heading. Maybe a holiday cottage, something like that you used to visit in the area when you were a kid?"

"Let me think it over. Jesus, why can't I remember?"

Lorne heard Sam telling Denis not to hit himself. She added her reassurance, "Denis, don't punish yourself for your parents' failings. Just relax. If it comes to you, then fine. If it doesn't, then we'll have to dig deep and work things out for ourselves."

"I'm letting you down. I'm letting everyone down. I want you to catch him before he harms anyone else."

"We'll get him, Denis. Can you pass the phone over to Sam for me?"

Sam came on the line, a note of distress in her voice. "Hello, Lorne."

"Hi, Sam. Please, you have to keep Denis calm. Think about when people are in a hypnotic state and how easily the information comes to them. We won't get anywhere if he remains stressed out. I've just told him that this Porter's car has been spotted on the way to Brighton. Does that ring a bell with you at all?"

Sam thought her question over and then replied, "No, nothing. I'm so sorry."

"Not to worry. I'm going to hang up now. I have another call waiting. I'll be in touch soon regarding Denis visiting the house, okay?"

"Thank you."

Lorne tapped a button on her phone and then another. "AJ, what's up?"

"Not sure how to tell you this, boss."

"Just say it!"

"We've got reports coming in about a hold-up going on at a petrol station."

"Don't tell me. Porter and Platt are involved, yes?"

"Yep. The thing is, they've taken off in another car. A faster car."

CHAPTER SEVENTEEN

Lorne and Sean debated what to do next. AJ had informed Lorne that several teams were already on their way to try to block and apprehend the vehicle Porter and Platt had stolen. The poor woman who owned the vehicle had left the scene by ambulance, after the men violently assaulted her when she refused to relinquish her keys.

"We've got two options as I see it," Lorne stated. "Either we join the circus and end up getting in each other's way, or we can take a backseat on that one and concentrate on finding more evidence to fling at the Platts."

Sean eased the car over into a layby and twisted in his seat to look at her. "You're talking about going to the house with Denis, right?"

"Absolutely. There's every chance he'll lead us to vital information, more clues as to what went on. If we're talking about cracking a paedophile ring, then we should definitely go down that route."

"I agree. You should call Denis and tell him to meet us at the house then."

Lorne dialled the number. The phone rang several times before Sam picked it up. "Sam, it's Lorne again. Is Denis there?"

"Yes. He's not doing so good right now, Lorne. Can I take a message?"

Crap! "Oh? Anything I can help with?"

"He's just sifting through the painful memories. Just a moment. He wants a word."

Lorne waited for Denis to come on the line, her stomach twisting into knots.

"Hello, Lorne."

"Denis, Sam told me that you're struggling at present. What can I do to help?"

"I don't think anyone can help really. My mind has to collate everything it has stored away for years and try to put it in some semblance of order."

"Okay, do you think meeting up at your parents' home is likely to hinder or help with that achievement?"

"I really can't answer that. Why are you ringing again so soon?"

"First of all, I wanted to inform you that we're on your father's tail. We believe he and Porter have held up a petrol station and stolen another vehicle, but we're on to them. They won't get far."

"Damn, was anyone hurt?"

"Yes, a lady, the owner of the car. She's being cared for in hospital. There's no need for you to worry about that, Denis."

He sighed heavily. "Easier said than done."

"I appreciate that. The second thing I wanted to run past you is whether you're up to going to the house now to meet us there?"

He paused a little while before he spoke again. "Okay, I suppose it would be better to get this over and done with as soon as possible."

"Brilliant. Do you want to make your own way over there? Or if you'd rather, we could make a detour and pick you up."

"No, I'm fine. Is it all right if Sam comes, too?"

"Of course, if you think that will help."

"It will. What time do you want us there?"

"How about in twenty minutes? Is that too soon?"

"That's fine. I'll just throw some cold water on my face. See you soon."

Lorne tucked her phone into her jacket pocket and leaned back against the headrest. "I can't say I'm looking forward to this."

"Why?"

"He sounds a mess. I can understand where he's coming from, wanting to get this task out of the way. I just don't think he realises how traumatic it's going to be for him."

"We'll be there to help him through the ordeal, Lorne."

"I know. Shit! I hope Patti will be all right about us turning up out of the blue. I better ring and warn her." Lorne started to fish her phone out of her pocket again but stopped when she saw Sean shaking his head out of the corner of her eye.

"I wouldn't do that if I were you. She'll probably object to us going there. The element of surprise is always preferable in such situations."

Lorne cringed. The last thing she wanted was to upset Patti by turning up unannounced and insisting on traipsing all over a crime scene.

Lorne jumped out of the car and entered the house. Thankfully, Denis and Sam hadn't arrived yet. Sean ran around the front of the car and was close on Lorne's heels by the time she walked through the front door.

"Leave the talking to me. I know how to handle her," Lorne said.

Sean grinned. "I had every intention of doing just that."

Lorne showed her ID to the officer standing in the hallway of the house, then she rushed through to the kitchen. The noise of several machines drifted up from the cellar. Lorne gulped and tentatively made her way down the stairs to the gruesome confines of the house. She called out when she reached the penultimate step, "Patti, are you here?"

A white-suited figure approached her. The person removed a blue paper mask and coughed. The air was full of dust particles that the equipment had disturbed. "Lorne? What are you doing here? I thought I said I would get back to you later."

"You did." Lorne's mouth twisted, and she clicked her tongue. "I have a dilemma."

"Concerning what?"

"Denis Platt contacted me about something he believes is in the loft. I've arranged to meet him and his girlfriend here. They're due any minute." Lorne could see Patti's foot start to tap as her friend folded her arms.

Shaking her head, Patti said, "Why? Why can't it wait?"

"He's in bits about this, Patti. He's finding the whole thing rather traumatic. I think it would be better to face all his demons as soon as he can."

"Does he know about what's going on down here?" Patti snapped at her.

"Yes and no. I've kept as much from him as possible. He knows about the original skeleton found in the cupboard, but that's it. Don't be angry with me, Patti. You know I wouldn't put you in this position ordinarily…"

"I know. I'm sorry for snapping. Put it down to pressure."

Lorne nodded her acceptance. "How's it going?"

"It's going. Eight bodies up until now."

"What? Eight? I know it's too early to speculate, but any idea about cause of death or the age of the victims?"

"COD, no can do on that at the moment. I can give you a guestimate of between five and fifteen for the ages. There's a mixture down here."

"Are they all skeletons? Or any recent additions?" Lorne glanced past Patti's left shoulder as two members of her team carefully placed some bones on a plastic sheet. One of the men jotted down information on his clipboard. Then they both crouched over the hole that had been dug in the corner of the room.

"No recent additions as far as we can tell. Saying that, we're going to have to dig up the garden, as well. That might alter things considerably, judging by what we've discovered in this small area."

"Crap! I don't suppose anyone has had a look in the attic yet, have they?"

"No." Patti's eyes widened in frustration. "Er... that'll be because we haven't had time yet."

"Sorry. Will you trust me up there?"

"I'm going to have to, aren't I? If you're that determined. And stop apologising when you don't really mean it."

"That's not fair. I *do* mean it."

"Hmm... make sure you're suitably attired. You'll find some suits in the boot of my car." Patti turned back to resume her examination of a victim's remains.

Lorne ascended the stairs to join Sean. "She's not happy about things but has given her blessing, nonetheless. Any sign of Denis and Sam yet?"

"Nope." He glanced at his watch and tapped the face with his finger. "They should be here any minute."

Lorne heard a noise in the hallway and saw Denis and Sam pushing open the front door. "Stay there," she shouted to the couple and added to the uniformed officer restraining them, "They're here to see us."

"Yes, ma'am." The officer dropped his arm.

Lorne smiled at Sean. "Here we go. I hope you're prepared for this. I know I'm not."

He motioned for her to go ahead of him up the hallway and whispered, "Only time will tell."

After Sean retrieved three sets of protective suits, boots, caps, and gloves from Patti's car, Lorne and Denis slipped into their ensembles. Then she took the lead up the stairs while Sean quickly put on his gear. "There should be a ladder up there," Denis informed them once they were all on the landing. "I'll have to get a stool from the bedroom." He hesitated before he walked into the master bedroom. He returned carrying a white-and-pink dralon-covered stool and placed it beneath the loft hatch. "Do you want me to go first?"

"I think I should. We need to be careful up there, careful not to disturb too much before the forensic team can conduct their investigation."

"Okay, I'll just pull down the ladder for you." Denis reached up and unhitched the latch holding the small door in place. He pulled down the metal ladder then stepped aside for Lorne to climb up.

She poked her head into the eerie loft space. She'd always hated going into lofts as a child, and she felt the same feelings of apprehension constricting her stomach muscles as the rungs of the ladder ran out. She stepped onto the boards of the loft. *Don't forget to breathe*, her inner voice yelled. "Okay, Denis, join me when you're ready." She flicked a nearby switch, and the room lit up.

Through the hatch, she saw Denis glance first at Sam then at Sean for reassurance before he began his ominous journey. Sam kissed him on the cheek and rubbed his arm. "You'll be fine. Lorne will be with you every step of the way."

Nodding, Denis bravely took the first steps up the ladder. It seemed a lifetime had passed before he completed his task to join Lorne. She helped him find his footing once he'd passed the end of the ladder, and together, they inhaled a large breath.

Lorne winked. Pushing her own uncertainties about her surroundings to one side for the moment, she told him, "You can do this, Denis."

"I hope so."

Lorne scanned the area. "When was the last time you were up here?"

"Not since I was nine or ten, I suppose." He closed his eyes as the memory took hold, and he shuddered.

"I'm here. Don't fret. I know this must be difficult for you. Be strong. Where shall we start? Was there anything in particular that you wanted me to see?"

Slowly, Denis's eyes opened. His gaze gradually surveyed the area amidst plenty of large gulps. "Things are different to how I remember. Give me a moment."

"Of course, in your own time. Let's move over here, away from the opening." The rustling of their suits as they tentatively crossed the boards had an unnerving effect over Lorne in the eerie environment. She had to dig deep to resist the urge to copy Denis's shudder moments earlier.

Denis studied each area carefully until his focus was drawn to a particular spot under the eaves. He surprised Lorne by reaching for and grabbing her gloved hand.

"This way," he whispered, leading her across the width of the room.

Lorne tried to look around his broad frame to figure out what they were heading for. All she could see were a pile of boxes and the odd suitcase tucked neatly away in a corner.

Stopping before one of the cases, Denis breathed in deeply and pointed. "In there. I think you'll find everything you're going to need in there."

Lorne stepped around him and walked toward the item. Pausing before she touched it, she asked, "What's in here, Denis?"

He shook his head. "I have no idea. All I know is that as a child I was forbidden from ever opening it. I tried once…"

"What happened, love?" Lorne prompted him to continue.

His hand swept over his pained face. "He beat me—every hour, on the hour for days, and he locked me in the cupboard under the stairs. I was in there for three whole days, not even allowed to leave to use the toilet."

"Denis, I'm so sorry. Let's hope we find the evidence we need in here on both of them to throw away the key."

"You have to find him first."

"We will. Would you rather I did this by myself?"

"No. I've come this far. I might as well continue now."

They both knelt, and Lorne flipped the brass-coloured catch on the front, surprised that it hadn't discoloured at all in the damp atmosphere. *Did that mean that Denis's parents constantly looked at its contents?* "Why isn't it locked? I mean, if they were determined that you kids shouldn't nosey inside it."

"Fear. They controlled us by fear. After what I went through, it kept the other kids in line. At the dinner table, on the days they actually fed us, they ridiculed me about the incident. That went on for years, not days or months, but years."

Lorne's eyes moistened not for the first time while in this gentle man's company. She'd heard some barbaric things over the years, even seen some of the most deplorable cases that had ever taken place in London, and yet this man's plight touched her like no other.

The thought of a mere child being treated so inhumanely by his parents completely saddened her. She wished Charlie were there with them so she could hug her daughter and tell her how much she was loved, but then her daughter knew that. Lorne had put her own life in jeopardy without a second thought over the years in order to save her only child. *That's how it should be with parents, not this!* No one had the right to treat kids the way the Platts had. Then Lorne thought about how lucky Denis was in reality—at least he was alive. There were around eight bodies in the cellar who hadn't survived the Platts' bouts of anger.

Lorne patted his arm and again apologised on his parents' behalf. "I'm sorry."

"I appreciate that, but it's not your fault. Let's get this over with." He urged her to open the case.

Lorne lifted the lid, looking through half-closed eyes, fearing what would present itself and whether either of them would be able to cope with the reveal. Instantly, she felt her stomach want to reject her lunch. *Oh, crap! Why me?* Images of dead battered children stared up at her. "Shit! Denis, don't look." When she turned to face him, he seemed to be in some form of mesmeric state. "Denis, listen to me, please."

Tears trickled down his cheeks, flowing more quickly the faster he shook his head. All of a sudden, he looked up at the roof and shouted, "*Why?*"

Lorne found it impossible not to cry. She threw her arms around him, and together, they sobbed. She heard the clatter of metal and looked over Denis's shoulder to see Sean poking his head through the hatch.

"Everything all right, Lorne?"

She waved her hand at him, released Denis, and wiped her eyes on the sleeve of her protective suit. "We'll be fine. Won't we, Denis?"

He nodded and gave Sean a thumbs-up. Reluctantly, Lorne's temporary partner left them to it and descended the ladder again.

Lorne held Denis by the shoulders. "Okay, we're going to force ourselves to do this. Or would you rather I looked through it myself?"

"No. We'll do this together. I can do this. I will confront what they've hidden from us all for years."

"Good man." She returned to the chore of sifting through the contents once more. She gathered all the photos of the children and placed them on the floor to the side of her. After Lorne removed the picture of the last child, what she revealed next, made Lorne want to vomit a second time. "Holy shit! Sick effing bastards!" Dozens and dozens of Kodak pictures of both Platts holding up dead animals filled her vision. It was Lorne's turn to look up at the roof and call out in a heart rendering cry, "Why?"

Denis gasped and ran his fingers over the pictures. "All my pets over the years. They killed them. Every time one went missing, they said that they'd visited the vets to put the animals to sleep, or in some cases said that the animals had run off. Nothing could be further from the truth. They killed them all."

"I run a rescue centre with my husband and daughter. I despise any form of animal abuse. You know what they say about serial killers, don't you?"

"I heard it on *CSI: Miami* the other night. Most of them begin by practising on animals."

Lorne picked up the photos and placed them in another pile beside her, wondering what their removal from the case would reveal next. Thankfully, beneath lay piles of documents. At first glance, Lorne could tell that most of the paperwork was to do with the couple's fostering obligations. "Birth certificates." She handed those to Denis.

"These are of my siblings. My sister Jill had the sense to get out when she was sixteen. Strange that she hasn't taken her birth certificate with her, don't you think?"

"Yes, she would have needed that to get on in life. When did she leave? Do you remember?"

He contemplated her question for a few seconds. "Around ten years ago."

"Has she been in touch since her departure?"

"No. I always thought it was because I had remained in contact with my parents and she disapproved of that."

"I'll see if we can track her down for you."

"That would be wonderful to be reunited with her. She suffered the most at *his* hands. He raped her constantly. I used to lay there every night, listening out for her muffled screams. There wasn't a night I didn't hear them."

"What happened the day she left?"

"Nothing. She packed a bag without saying anything to any of us and just left."

"Who could blame her after going through that ordeal? I think I would have done the same, given the circumstances."

Denis nodded and looked down at the certificates again. He paused and took a closer look at the next one in the pile. "It's mine." His gaze met Lorne's, his eyes the size of dinner plates. "I don't have the same name as my parents."

"What?" Lorne snatched the cream-coloured sheet from his hand and looked for herself.

"What does this mean? That I'm adopted?"

"I have no idea. Now we have this, we can do some digging. Tell me if the other certificates seem in order?"

Denis quickly riffled through the rest of them then placed them in his lap. "They appear to be okay."

"Good, at least that's some good news." Lorne searched the case again and pulled out a small hard-backed notebook. "What's this?"

Denis shrugged. "Open it and see."

Lorne flipped open the first page. It seemed to be in date order. There were names and addresses, although the addresses appeared to be shortened, as if they were in code. She would have to delve into that once she was back at the station. The dates ran from 1995. Lorne flicked through the sheets to the end of the book and almost dropped it when she saw the previous week's date. She had already guessed what she was witnessing. This was a record of abuse.

Denis grabbed the book from her hand and turned to the front of it again. He prodded at a name on the page. "I know him... he was a frequent visitor to the house."

Lorne swallowed before she asked, "Did he abuse you, Denis?"

"Yes. He raped all of us at one time or another."

Lorne gently relieved him of the book again. "This is all the evidence we need to literally throw the book at them. We've got it. Be happy in the knowledge that they will never see the light of day again, Denis. Never."

Denis shook his head. "But you haven't got Platt, Lorne. Look at that book, the names, the contacts he has. One or all of those people listed will hide him if he asked them to. You'll never find him." He ran a distraught gloved hand through his hair, wincing as the plastic pulled some hair from the roots.

"Nonsense. We're so close to him right now. Please, Denis, don't give up on us. Everyone tracking him is aware of how dangerous he is. They'll do everything they can to prevent him from escaping a second time."

"I hope you're right, Lorne. I dread to think of the consequences if he does manage to get away."

Lorne nodded solemnly. "Let's gather this lot together and get out of here, yes?"

Denis's gaze homed in on another suitcase, and he pointed at it. "Can we look in here first?"

"Of course." Lorne shuffled across the boards on her knees and flicked a similar catch on the second suitcase. "*Shit!*" She shouted as she revealed the contents and stumbled backwards.

"Shit!" Denis mumbled as he caught her.

CHAPTER EIGHTEEN

Neither Lorne nor Denis could hold back the vomit when they realised what they'd stumbled across. The skeleton had belonged to an infant child. Anyone would be able to work that out without the need of a pathologist's expert view.

Sean rushed up the ladder again and entered the attic space. He peered over Lorne's shoulder and gasped. "Jesus!"

"We need to get out of here, Sean. Leave everything as it is and call Patti up here."

The three of them climbed back down the ladder, each visibly shaking from head to toe.

"What is it? You look as though you've seen a ghost," Sam said, throwing an arm around Denis's waist to support him.

Denis buried his head in his hands, and muffled words tumbled out of his mouth, "It's all up there, even the remains of one of the children."

"No! Oh, Denis, I'm so sorry." Sam kissed his cheek.

Lorne and Sean left the couple and ran down the stairs and into the basement. "Patti. Sorry to interrupt, but you'll want to hear this."

Patti groaned as she stood and marched over to them. "I am busy here, Lorne, in case you haven't noticed."

"I know, I know! You need to do a thorough search of the loft, too."

Patti tilted her head. "Enlighten me? Not that I wasn't going to do that anyway."

"We just found an infant's skeleton shoved in a suitcase. There could be more. I didn't get a chance to search everywhere. I thought it imperative to get everyone out of there ASAP."

"I'm glad to hear it. Damn, how many frigging more are we going to find?"

"I dread to think. We've found a book with a list of names, addresses, and amounts in it. I'm thinking it was some kind of record of abuse. Denis confirmed that he was regularly abused by one man on the first page of the book. Can your guys note it down as evidence? I need to take it with me, though, if that's okay? I promise no one will touch it without gloves on."

"Very well, it's obviously an important part of your investigation. Jesus, we're talking about some warped fucking people here, aren't we?"

"And this is just the beginning. There's a bunch of birth certificates up there, too. My take is that you'll be able to match up some of the remains to them. Here's another thing—Denis found his certificate and has just discovered he has a different name."

"Did he go through the system? Did they adopt him?"

"Not that he can remember. He's always regarded the Platts as his own mother and father. It was a total shock to him. That poor man, and then to witness what he's just seen... I can't begin to imagine what's going through his mind at the moment."

Patti shook her head. "Talking of fathers, any news on him?"

"I'm just going to ring the station now, although I think they would have informed me if he'd been caught."

"Okay, let's get this noted down, and then you can leave. Mick, can you deal with this for me?"

The technician stepped forward, clipboard in hand, and noted the evidence, then he placed it in an envelope for Lorne.

"Thanks. I'll be in touch soon."

Sam and Denis had made their way downstairs and were standing in the hallway when Lorne and Sean returned to the kitchen. "Do you think we should take them into protective custody until Platt is found?" Lorne asked.

"Maybe that wouldn't be a bad idea, in light of what we've just uncovered. I'll get onto it when we get back to the station. They can accompany us. They'll be safer there than at their flat."

"I'll see if they're agreeable. You could always try and make the arrangements from your car. It'll save some time." Lorne smiled and winked at him.

"Okay. Give me ten minutes and then join me. The sooner we get back, the better."

"I'll tell them. Be with you soon."

Sean stripped off his suit and left the house. Lorne took Sam and Denis into the lounge, where she and Denis discarded the used suits into a black bag.

Lorne explained what she and Sean had discussed. "Is that all right with you both? You'll be safer, and I'll have peace of mind knowing that you're safe."

Denis held Sam's hand tightly. Together, they nodded. "I think it's for the best, until he's behind bars," Denis agreed.

"That's great news. My boss is sorting that out now. He should have it sorted within the next few minutes—"

Her mobile rang and she strode out to the hallway to take the call. "AJ? Tell me it's good news. I couldn't handle anymore shit right now."

"It is, boss. They've caught them. Platt and Porter. They're being transported to the remand centre now."

"Thank God for that. Any casualties?"

"A few men with cuts and bruises, nothing major. The same can't be said for the suspects, though. They'll need a spell in the remand centre's hospital wing for a day or two." AJ sniggered.

"Saved me a job of beating the crap out of them," Lorne replied, relief flooding through every vein. "We'll be back soon. Any news on the warrant for those files yet?"

"More good news I wanted to tell you about. It came through around fifteen minutes ago. I've sent Stephen and Graham over there to pick the files up. Hope that was okay?"

"Brilliant! Well done, you. See you in a while."

Lorne hung up, poked her head round the lounge door, and told the hugging couple, "They've got him. We've got him. You're safe, at last." Then she left the elated couple and went outside to the car. Lorne motioned for Sean to end his call.

He hopped out of the car and frowned. "Why? Have they got him?"

"Yes. I've informed Denis and Sam. There's no need for you to organise the safe house now."

"Brilliant. Back to the station now, yes?"

"Yep. One last thing I need to tell Patti. I'll be with you in two minutes."

Lorne flew down the stairs as if she'd grown a pair of eagle wings. Patti was as relieved as Lorne to hear the news of Platt's arrest, and she promised to ring Lorne later that evening with an update.

The incident room had a different aura about it when Lorne and Sean arrived twenty minutes later. Stephen and Graham were right behind them, carrying a bulging archive box full of files.

"Jesus! How many kids have these guys fostered over the years?" Lorne asked, shaking her head, her eyes misting up easily again.

Stephen shrugged. "We won't know until we begin sifting through this lot."

Lorne looked at the clock on the wall—it was almost seven o'clock. "Okay, I need to take a vote. Who's up for pulling an all-nighter? I'll dip my hand in my pocket and supply a takeaway later for those willing to stay."

"No, you won't. I will," Sean butted in, raising his hand. "Come on, guys, anyone else willing to give up their comfortable evening and warm bed?"

"If you put it like that, I'm in," AJ said.

The rest of the team followed suit, and Lorne's chest puffed up with pride. However, it quickly deflated when she realised she would have to ring home and break the news to Tony.

Sean nudged her in the back. "Go on, get it out of the way."

Lorne went through to Katy's office and closed the door. Picking up the landline, she rang home.

Tony answered after the first ring, as if he'd been waiting for her call. "Hi, love. How was your day?" Lorne asked.

"Frustrating. Yours?"

"Gratifying, heart-breaking. It swung between both of them, really. Umm… I need to pull an all-nighter."

"What? You're winding me up, right?"

"No, sorry. What we've uncovered is absolutely deplorable, Tony. If I didn't stay here and thrash my way through it, I wouldn't be able to shut off my mind and sleep anyway."

"Shit! Really? It's that bad?"

"It honestly is. I'll make it up to you at the weekend, I promise."

"I'll hold you to that. Charlie just told me how excited she is about having time off and going away. I thought then that she wouldn't be the only one."

"Cheeky. Okay, better fly. See you tomorrow."

"Ouch, that sounds awful."

"Yeah, forget I said that. See you in a few hours. Love you."

"Love you, too."

Lorne walked back into the incident room. The first thing that caught her eye was how unhappy Sean looked when he hung up the phone.

"Carmen's not a happy bunny, I take it?"

"Hardly, the baby has been playing up all day with teething pains. I feel guilty as bloody sin now."

"Damn, sorry to hear that. She would have been looking forward to you doing the nightshift there, instead of here."

"Never mind. We'll get over it. What's first on the agenda?"

"I need to get the team searching the net for research purposes then. If you like, we can tackle that pile of files together?"

"Do I have a choice?"

"Nope, I'm *Acting* DI, remember? You're my partner."

"Thought you might remind me of that one. Glad you didn't disappoint."

"Okay, attention please, peeps. Has everyone cleared it with home?" Lorne's gaze swept across the room, and everyone nodded. "Great stuff. First of all, I need everyone to wear gloves when handling what's in the envelope. Is that clear? Okay, AJ and Karen, I need you to see what you can dig up about the children using their birth certificates, all right?"

"Are we likely to find anything?" AJ asked, looking puzzled.

"I have no idea, AJ. All I know is that some of the certs go back years. They're not all concerning recent foster children. Just see how you go, okay? Karen, I want you to look at one in particular for me."

"Ma'am?"

"The one belonging to Denis, the Platts' son. His birth certificate leads me to think they're not his real parents. See what you can do for me?"

Karen sighed and shook her head in disgust. "I'll do my very best."

Lorne knew she would. "Stephen and Graham, I need you to go through this book. Try and decipher the addresses and let me have a list of the people noted down and whether they're still around or not. Glancing through, I thought I spotted a few famous names in there. I hope I'm mistaken, but in light of the Jimmy Savile case, I'm not prepared to discount anyone from our enquiry at this point."

"Okay, we'll see what we can find out."

Lorne went to lift the box of files onto the desk, but Sean, being the gentleman he was, pulled her aside and heaved it onto the desk beside her.

"I think we need more room." She pulled the chairs out from underneath a few of the other tables and pushed three tables together.

"That should do." She sighed deeply enough for her cheeks to puff out. "Right, where do we begin?"

"At the beginning," Sean said, ducking to avoid the inevitable swipe coming his way from Lorne.

She gave him a cheesy grin, a little light relief before they sank their teeth into the onerous task ahead of them. "Go and do something useful—buy us all a coffee."

By the time Sean had bought and handed out the drinks to the team, Lorne had placed the files on the desks in date order. She opened a couple of files, and a frequent name jumped off the page at her. "Stephen, look out for this name—Sid Weston."

"Nothing as yet, boss."

"Okay, tell me right away if you find anything."

Sean's expression was one of confusion. "Why that name in particular?"

"Something Denis said about social workers being involved." Lorne turned the file in front of her in his direction and pointed out the man's name. "Here. I've already seen his name and signature on several other files, too."

"Beggar's belief that someone in that role can be linked to such heinous crimes against children."

"Truthfully, nothing surprises me after what I've heard in the last few years. I wish capital punishment was still an option in this country. We need a deterrent of sorts. The gallows sounds a good enough one to me."

"I can't disagree with you there, Lorne."

"If I had my way, anyone tampering with kids would be hanged as soon as they were arrested. There's no smoke and all that."

After an exhausting night, Lorne breezed through her tiredness and glanced around at her team. They'd done her proud. Each and every one of them had pulled out all the stops and achieved more than was expected of them in a working week, let alone twelve hours. Sean sent Graham for bacon rolls, and while they ate their breakfast, they summed up what they'd established so far. An adrenaline rush had pushed away any tiredness Lorne had expected to feel.

She walked over to the incident board. "Right, let's try and make some sense of this." She took a bite of her roll and pointed at AJ. "You start, AJ."

"I've managed to locate some of the children they fostered in the system, but there are so many that I think it's going to take me a full week to track all of them down—if they're trackable, that is."

"Okay, I'm not expecting miracles, so a few is a great start. At this point, I'm mainly interested in one in particular. Karen, any luck?"

Karen's tired eyes met Lorne's, and she smiled. "Just doing final checks now, but I think I've hit the jackpot."

Lorne's heart skipped several beats. "Really? That's fantastic news. Well, between the rest of us, we've been appalled by what we've unearthed. The magnitude of this case has just gone through the roof and half way to the moon. The people, if you can call them that—I'd rather they were known as animals—have been fairly easy to identify, thanks to the way the Platts have listed them. Was that intentional on their part? Probably, I wouldn't put it past them to do everything they could to implicate all concerned. None of them can be labelled as having morals, any of them. So, we have an extensive list of depraved human beings in some very high-profiled positions, including apparently the head of social services at the time. Sick shits, the lot of them! The chief even spotted a former superintendent in another force amongst the visitors to the house. Fortunately for him, he's no longer with us. We'll pass all the information onto the Paedophile Unit, let them deal with the lowlifes while we concentrate on the three murders of the tradesmen, for now, until Patti has identified the remains at the house."

Sean nodded. "Good idea. I'd like to say something, if I may?"

Lorne propped her backside on the nearest desk. "Be my guest."

"I'd just like to add my congratulations to the team for what you achieved last night. All of you have gone above and beyond on this one. I want to personally thank you for that. Lorne and Katy are always singing your praises, and after working with you closely this past week, I can totally understand why. I am extremely proud and honoured to have such a devoted and professional team working under me."

Lorne smiled and vigorously nodded her agreement. "Hear, hear." She clapped. "I couldn't have said it better myself."

At five o'clock that evening, Lorne shooed the team home. Some of them, notably AJ, showed their disdain for being ordered to go home, while others looked relieved to call it a day after their thirty-two-hour shift. She pulled into the drive and got out of the car. Leaning against the closed door, she shut her eyes and raised her face to the warm evening sun, letting the slight breeze tickle her skin.

"Hey, you." Hearing Tony's voice came as a welcome relief. He kissed her. "You haven't got time to take in the sun's rays."

"Haven't I? Why?"

"I want my dinner."

Lorne shook her head. "Charming! After the long shift I've just embarked upon, you're expecting me to come home and cook!"

He shrugged. "Unless you fancy burnt offerings again for dinner?"

"Where's Charlie?"

"Packing. She'll be leaving in a little while for her weekend away."

"Damn, is it Friday already?"

"Yes, Lorne. Come on. I have some news for you."

Lorne hesitated before walking towards the house. "Is this good or bad news?"

"Both. I'll tell you over a coffee."

Charlie was sitting at the kitchen table, stroking Sheba when they entered the back door. "Hi, Mum, I hope it was worth it."

"The long shift? Definitely. Are you ready for the off?" Lorne noticed the overnight bag at her daughter's feet.

"Yep, just having a final cuddle with Sheba. I wish she was coming with me. You will look after her over the weekend, won't you? You won't be spending *all* your time in bed, I hope?"

Lorne laughed. "Not at our age, love. She'll be fine with us."

"I'm going to take off now and leave you to it then. Have fun, kiddos." Charlie hugged Lorne then Tony. She pulled away and wagged her finger. "Nine months down the line, I don't want to be hearing the patter of tiny feet around the place. You hear me?"

"You cheeky mare, I should be saying that to you, not the other way around. Anyway, I couldn't take the stress of having another child as demanding as you running around the place."

"Who's the cheeky one? Hmm… we'll see. Love you," she called over her shoulder and ran out the back door, leaving a forlorn-looking Sheba staring after her.

Lorne sat in the chair Charlie had just vacated and proceeded to pet Sheba while Tony made a coffee.

When Tony joined her at the table, Lorne said, "Okay, I want the good news first."

He looked down at his mug. "We solved the case."

"That's brilliant news. Today?"

"No, yesterday."

Lorne frowned. "Why didn't you tell me when I rang last night?"

"Be fair. I didn't really get the chance to."

"I'm sorry, love. I feel guilty now."

He placed his hand on top of hers. "There's no need."

"Okay, what's the bad news?"

"He's dead. We fished Alec Edmonds out of the river."

Lorne gasped. "Oh no. That's terrible. Was it foul play, do you suspect?"

"We don't think so. Looks like he lost his footing and fell into the river. He was intoxicated, remember. Of course, we're waiting on the pathologist's report to verify that. Poor bloke."

"I bet his fiancée was distraught, wasn't she?"

"I ended up calling for a doctor to sedate her."

"I'd be the same if I ever I lost you, Tony."

He leaned over and kissed her. "Do you want to show me how much I mean to you upstairs?"

Lorne hesitated, her stomach growling through hunger. "Crap, can we eat first?"

"It's all in hand. Come with me, young lady." He locked the back door and grabbed her hand as he passed, pulling her upstairs behind him. He pushed open the bedroom door. The bed was covered in pink and red rose petals, and on top of the quilt was a tray filled with oysters, strawberries, and champagne. *I guess I won't be going hungry after all.*

CHAPTER NINETEEN

After spending a restful, romantic weekend with Tony, Lorne ventured into work on Monday morning on a high.

AJ was at his desk, as usual, when she walked into the incident room.

"How's things? Have you heard from Katy?"

"Did I hear my name mentioned?"

Lorne turned to face her partner and crossed the floor to hug her. "You're back. That's stating the obvious, I know. I take it your dad's all right now?"

Katy smiled. "He is. Not fully out of the woods yet. The hospital said he needs a heart operation to unblock a few valves. They're keeping him stable, and he's improving daily, so Mum insisted I should come back to work."

"That's great news."

Katy ran a hand over her face. Lorne grabbed it and pulled it towards her. "What's this?" She stared at the glistening diamond sitting on Katy's ring finger.

"Doh! What does it look like, numpty?"

AJ left his desk and joined them. He threw an arm around Katy's waist. "I asked Katy to marry me before she went to Manchester. She was mulling it over when she got the call from her mum."

Lorne placed a hand over her chest. "So that's what was on your mind. Jesus, I had a horrible feeling for a minute there that you were pregnant."

Katy and AJ quickly glanced at each other and started to laugh. "We are!" they said in unison.

"What?" Lorne fell into a nearby chair and stared at them both, her mouth hanging open.

"You don't look overjoyed by the news, Lorne," Katy said, looking concerned.

"But... but what about your job?"

Katy raised an eyebrow. "You coped all right raising a child and being an inspector at the same time."

"Urm... hardly! I hate to dash your dreams, but actually, I didn't. Tom raised Charlie. He was a stay-at-home dad, if you remember."

"We'll cross that bridge when we come to it. We have a few months yet before we are forced to make any drastic decisions on that front."

"Whatever Katy decides to do is okay with me," AJ added, supporting his fiancée.

"I'll add my support if you need it, too. You know that," Lorne added, not sure if she actually meant the sentiment or not.

The rest of the team arrived, drawing a halt to their conversation. Karen called Lorne over to her desk not long after their shift began. "Here you go. I think you've been waiting for this."

Lorne looked down at the scrap of paper on which Karen had scribbled a name and address. "Thanks, Karen. You're a star." She walked into Katy's office and stood in the doorway, shuffling her feet.

"Go on, out with it," her partner said.

"Do you mind if I pop out for an hour or so? It's to do with the case, I promise."

"Okay, I'll be tied up with this shit for a while anyway. One thing before you go—the remand centre where Mrs. Platt is residing at present just rang me."

Lorne flopped into the chair. "And? Has she tried to top herself?"

"Nothing like that. She requested to speak to a psychiatrist over the weekend."

"Surprise, surprise. I had a feeling she'd try and pull that one."

"Hear me out, Lorne. The woman made a full confession about all the murders, the tradesmen and the kids."

"Never! Really? Can we get her to repeat that in a statement? You know we can't use anything she says to a doc, don't you?"

"I'm aware of that. Now, shut up and listen. First, she said the electrician, plumber, and the plasterer were all killed because they discovered the skeleton in the cupboard, plus they all pissed her off by talking constantly to her about their wonderfully happy families."

"Jesus! What a twisted sick bitch. What about the kids whose remains are yet to be identified? Is she willing to give us their names? That will save us months of trying to identify them."

Katy nodded. "They're going to work on her about that. She did offer us one of the identities, though—that of the skeleton in the cupboard."

"Who does it belong to?"

"Denis's sister. Or the person he grew up thinking was his sister, Jill."

"No! That's going to come as a bloody shock to him. He thought she'd packed her bags and left for greener pastures."

"Here's the clincher. When the psychiatrist asked her why they killed all the kids, her reply was it was all Denis's fault."

"What? Why? Christ, this just keeps getting better. Go on, surprise me."

"They blamed him because he refused to *die*."

Lorne sat back in her chair and covered her mouth with a hand. Tears sprang to her eyes. Dropping her hand, she whispered, "They're insane. There is no other word for their state of mind, is there?"

"Yeah, I was thinking along the same lines. Let's just hope they don't try and pull that card when they go to trial. Are you all right?"

"I will be. Can I shoot off now?"

"Go. Drive carefully."

Lorne pulled up outside the small terraced house and knocked on the door. The woman in her early fifties had a worn, kind-looking face. She seemed anxious to meet Lorne, but after Lorne assured her everything would be okay, the woman finally agreed to accompany her to Denis's house.

Sam opened the door to Lorne and raised a questioning eyebrow. "Hi, Sam. Is Denis up to receiving visitors?"

"I'm not sure. He's still devastated by what he found in the loft the other day. We've had a horrendous weekend. He's wracked with guilt, Lorne."

She patted Sam on the forearm and winked. "I wouldn't be here if I didn't think this visit would help him recover."

"Is she some kind of therapist?" Sam asked, looking at the woman standing apprehensively alongside Lorne.

"In a way." She winked again and added, "Trust me. Have I let you down before?"

"No, you haven't. Okay, come upstairs."

With each step they took, Lorne's heart beat faster. Finally, they entered the lounge.

Denis was sitting on the sofa, flipping through an old photo album. He looked up and tilted his head, seeming surprised to see Lorne standing there.

He rose from his seat and shook her hand. "Hello, Lorne. What are you doing here?"

"Hello, love. I think you better sit down again."

He did as she suggested. Lorne linked arms with the woman and steered her gently across the room. "Denis, I'd like you to meet your mum."

The two people stared at each other for a second or two. Then Denis's mother dropped to her knees in front of him and held out her arms.

Without hesitating, he fell into them. "Is it true? You're my real mother?"

"Yes, darling. I've been searching for you for the last twenty-nine years. They stole you from me."

"When? How?"

"One step at a time. Let's just rejoice at being reunited after all these years."

Lorne kissed Sam on the cheek and waved farewell before quietly sneaking out of the room. She prayed that all the arduous memories Denis had stored in his mind would dwindle into obscurity once he realised how powerful a real mother's love truly was. His healing would take time, but Lorne had every faith that the kind and gentle man would one day recover fully from his torturous ordeal, with Sam and his real mother by his side.

NOTE TO THE READER

Dear Reader,

Go on, be honest, I bet you shed a tear or two. I'm not too ashamed to tell you I did while writing Dubious Justice. Especially whilst writing the attic scene.

It's going to take Lorne a few weeks to get over such a traumatic case.

But her latest adversary has other plans in Calculated Justice.

It involves a deadly game of cat and mouse!

The clock is ticking to rescue several families who have been kidnapped.

Maybe you'll be able to lend a hand solving all the clues ahead of Lorne!

Grab your copy today.

https://melcomley.blogspot.co.uk/p/calculated-justice.html

Thank you for your continued support of my work, it truly means the world to me.

M A Comley

Sprinkle a little fairy dust in my direction by considering leaving a review if you will.

Made in United States
North Haven, CT
13 February 2023

32520712R00098